The Blue Rose

by Bill Muir

The Blue Rose

Bill Muir

Methinx Publishing

MeThinx Publishing

This novel is entirely a work of fiction. The names, characters, places, and incidents portrayed in it are the work of the author's imagination. Any resemblance to actual persons, living or dead, or real events or locations, is entirely coincidental.

Methinx Publishing
methinxentertainment.com

Printed in the United States of America
First paper edition by Methinx Publishing
ISBN: 978-1-7347696-5-4

Art & Design:
Contributing Editor: Kathryn Tedrick
Cover Art: Digital Coast Media, LLC

Prologue

Sixteen-year-old Arturo Espinoza ran out of a stunning white hacienda set into an oasis of green grass and surrounded by fields of roses as far as the eye could see. Handsome in his school uniform, he glanced back over his shoulder and sighed. He had escaped unnoticed this time, and his dark brown eyes danced in triumph. Reaching the gate and stepping through, he ran into brown-skinned, shabbily dressed Rolando Vasquez. Although the boys were the same age, it was one of the few things they had in common, along with their friendship. Financially, their families were as different as night and day.

They stared at each other for a beat before exchanging a practiced handshake, finishing off with a chest bump.

"Que pasa?" Arturo asked.

"This way," Rolando replied.

They ran off together into the nearby woods.

***

Arturo paced alone along the bank of a lake, located on the other side of the woods. The beautiful blue sky reflected in the clear water with glints of sunlight sparkling on gentle waves. The boys had gotten separated, and Rolando was nowhere in sight. Across the lake, twelve-year-old Rosa Gonzales peeked shyly from behind the trunk of a red oak tree. Her hair was dark and unclean, and she wore a simple blue dress. The slender fingers of her right-hand nervously held a perfect red rose.

Unaware that he was being watched, Arturo loosened and removed his tie, socks, and highly polished shoes and laid them in the grass nearby. Then rolling up his pant legs, he stepped barefooted into the shallow part of the lake and wiggled his toes in the cool sand. He smiled and sighed as the water washed over his feet and lower legs. It was a perfect day, and he took in the water and the sky and rejoiced at his temporary freedom, unaware that someone now stood a few feet behind him. Closing his eyes, he relaxed, until a strange feeling came over him that sent a prickle of danger up his spine. Someone was watching him. Arturo spun around, slipped in the mud, lost his footing and fell on his backside.

"Ah!"

Sitting there in the water, he realized that his fancy pants were soaked. He looked up, ready to yell at whoever had snuck up on him, only to find Rosa standing there serious as a soldier, holding out a hand to help him up.

"Oops. I am so sorry," Rosa apologized. "I did not mean to startle you."

Surprised to see this unknown girl instead of Rolando, he laughed and accepted her help to stand up.

"It's okay," he said. "My name's Arturo." He twisted slightly and turned his head to look at his rear. "And my butt isn't usually this wet."

"I know," Rosa's face flamed red. "I mean...about your name! Not your butt." She tried to swallow her mortification. "I'm your neighbor." She pointed across the lake. If she weren't so embarrassed, she might have laughed.

Arturo bowed slightly. "Nice to meet you."

Summoning her courage, she held out the rose. "I have wanted to give you this for a long time."

They stood frozen for a moment. Arturo looked surprised. Rosa was holding out the rose, her eyes staring at the ground. Finally, he stepped forward and smiled kindly.

"Is that one of the worker girls?" The voice of one of two pretty girls the same age as Arturo said as they emerged from the trees.

"Oh gross," the second girl said. "She's trying to give him a flower."

They both laughed and mumbled a few more unkind remarks.

Embarrassed, Rosa withered under their poking fun at her and their laughter, but Arturo stepped in front of her.

"Hey, leave her alone," he retorted.

"Chill, Arturo, we're just kidding," the first girl said, laughing dismissively.

Tears welled up in Rosa's eyes, and she ran away along the lakeside. Arturo turned and was about to follow when he heard the voice of his friend.

"I told you I would get 'em," Rolando said. He lumbered noisily out from the trees behind the girls. They giggled as he pulled off his shirt and rushed past them to splash through the shallow water and jump into the deeper part of the lake.

"Let's get this party started!" he called. "Oh! Cold! Mistake!"

The girls ran into the water after him, laughing and screaming when the cold water hit their warm skin. Arturo briefly watched them, and by the time he looked back to the lakeside, Rosa had left.

"Arturo! Where are you? The water's fine once you get used to it." He laughed. "By the looks of your pants, you already did."

His words brought more laughter from the girls.

Still looking along the lake, Arturo reluctantly unbuttoned his shirt. He was all for having fun and cooling off on a hot day, but he was still disturbed by the way the girls had made fun of Rosa. Was it because of her age? It didn't matter. It wasn't right.

Back in her hiding place behind the red oak tree, Rosa watched him step into the water and wade out towards the others. The girls welcomed him with laughter and splashes, and before long, he forgot about the shy little girl who had a crush on him. She had waited so long and lost so many opportunities to approach Arturo with her offering. Broken-hearted, she cried harder now and turned away from the sight of the four of them having so much fun. She had dropped the rose from her hand to the ground, where it lay after being crushed underneath her foot as she ran away.

Chapter One

Early one morning at the El Dorado International Airport located in Bogota, Colombia, a bright-eyed young flower girl waved a bouquet of blue roses back and forth, trying to entice the passersby to buy them. Spying a businessman in a white suit rushing her way, she stepped in front of him. "Roses, senor? Only $20."

"Out of my way," the man shouted. He didn't even bother to slow down but knocked the flower girl to the ground. Since she was poor, she was meaningless to him, not worthy of his attention. Stepping to the curb, he was about to flag a taxi when he noticed a beautiful lady standing further down along the curb.

"That's a shame, amigo."

The businessman turned to see Arturo, wearing a nicely pressed suit and highly polished shoes with designer luggage slung over his shoulder. "Excuse me?" He asked, annoyed.

"You missed an opportunity," Arturo told him. "Do you see what the flower girl is selling?"

"What do I care what she's selling? She is just another beggar, as far as I'm concerned. A plague on our streets that needs to be dealt with so that they don't bother honest, hard-working citizens like us."

Arturo raised one eyebrow. "Look closer." He did not like people who treated those less fortunate than themselves so poorly.

With a disgusted sigh, the businessman glanced at the girl. "Blue roses, so what?"

Arturo shook his head sadly. "She is selling romance, amigo. Roses aren't naturally blue when they are grown. They have to be dyed that way."

"What are you…a florist?"

Arturo smiled. "I grew up on a rose farm, and I can tell you that if you want to get someone's attention, you should hand her one of those and say, "A blue rose means that anything is possible."

The businessman glanced back at the flower girl again, who had recovered and was back on her feet. "Hey, how much are those?"

"She said, $50," Arturo said hurriedly. "Great deal."

The businessman pulled out a fifty and handed it to her. Snatching the flowers from her hand, he headed toward the lady.

The flower girl was thrilled, and her eyes shone brightly. "Gracias, senor!"

"You're welcome." Arturo winked. "Now, you had best take off before he sees what those do to his nice suit."

They turned to watch the businessman try and fail to impress the lady, who took one look at him and wrinkled her pert nose. He had not noticed the blue smears all over his white jacket yet.

The flower girl's eyes widened, and with a nod to Arturo, she ran off.

"You always were a charmer."

Arturo turned to find a chubby man in work clothes holding a sign that read: *Arturo Espinoza*. They stared at each other for a beat, then they did a practiced handshake, finished off with a chest bump.

"Que pasa, ñero?"

Rolando laughed, and then scooped his friend up in a big bear hug. "You look great, Arturo."

"Good to see you, Rolando."

"Man, ten years! You look like a different person. Business school, check! Congratulations."

"Gracias. What are you doing here?" Arturo asked.

"I'm the foreman at your dad's farm, and sometimes..." He made a motion with his hands like they were on a steering wheel. "I'm also his driver. This way, ñero." He grabbed Arturo's bags and headed toward the parking lot, talking the entire time. "I'm glad we have the whole drive to catch up. I can't wait to hear about your life in America. How's the food up there? I hear it's bad."

Rolando did not notice Arturo, who got into the car and sat behind him. His smile faded as he brushed the dust off his jacket.

***

A young couple entered a flower shop that they thought was charming. Cozy and welcoming, it only sold roses, and everywhere you looked, you saw a rainbow of colors – every color that is, but blue. The couple looked around before proceeding to the counter to speak with Abuela Jacqui, a 75-year-old woman who, despite her age, was still full of life, pluck, and had a sparkle in her eyes.

She looked from one to the other, and then said to the man, "What kind of roses would you like to give the beautiful senorita?"

The young man smiled. "Yellow, a dozen, please."

9

Jacqui gave him a knowing look and walked over to one of the buckets filled with water and roses. She took out a dozen fiery orange ones and walked back to the counter to wrap them in the paper.

Puzzled, the man said, "I'm sorry. I ordered yellow roses."

Abuela Jacqui smiled sweetly. "That's all right, dear. Nobody's perfect." She finished wrapping the paper around the flowers, put a small piece of scotch tape on the seam, and pushed them into his hands.

Confused, the young man looked from the flowers he held to Jacqui. "But yellow is her favorite color."

"Oh, sweetheart, yellow means friendship. Is that what you're after, or were you planning to round the bases tonight?"

The young man glanced at the young lady, who raised her eyebrows. "Answer the woman," she teased.

Before he could say another word, Rosa, who had heard the whole conversation, came through the back door that led into the rear of the shop, which had been left open. She was dressed in work attire and an apron. Her thick, long hair was pulled back into a ponytail. "Abuela Jacqui, can I get your help in the back?"

"Of course, Rosa." As Rosa gently escorted her grandmother away from the counter, Jacqui shook her head. "If your grandpa had given me yellow roses, your mother would never have been born."

Once Jacqui was through the door and headed for the task her granddaughter wanted her to do, Rosa grabbed a yellow bouquet and quickly wrapped it up. "Here you go. Yellow roses to the smart man who always knows to give the lady what she wants."

"Gracias." He handed the orange bouquet back, along with the money to pay for the ones he wanted. Then taking the yellow roses, he turned to the young lady. "For my best friend."

While Rosa unwrapped the orange roses and placed them back into a bucket of water, the couple walked out hand-in-hand. Smiling warmly, she watched them go. It was moments like these that made her world go around.

The only other customer in the store was handsome Pedro, a short, thin, thirty-year-old man with a very thick head of hair and a ready smile. "Hola, Rosa. How are you today?"

"I'm good, Pedro. It's always a beautiful day here at the shop. You want the usual?"

"You know me so well," he teased, doing his best to charm her.

Rosa began making his arrangement with practiced movements, gently and skillfully creating beauty right before his eyes. She selected different colored roses along with ferns and baby's breath. Pedro, however, wasn't looking at the flowers. He admired her looks, her figure, and watched her long, slender fingers as they worked their magic.

"It's not hard. You always get the same thing," she said without looking up. "Have you ever thought about trying something different?"

Pedro shrugged. "When you have found something perfect, why change?" He wasn't talking about the flowers, though.

Finished with her creation, Rosa handed him the arrangement. Pedro paid and exited the shop with a nod, walking past sassy Bella Velasquez as she stormed in, pulling her hair back into a ponytail and heading behind the counter to put an apron on over her impressive, hourglass figure.

"Sorry, I'm late! Rolando's truck is acting up. I barely made it at all."

"And only two hours late. Did you push it here?" Rosa asked teasingly.

"*You* try living with a house full of boys. Toilet was backed up this morning and wouldn't flush until I pulled 97 Legos out of it." She nodded toward the front door. "So, when are you going to say, yes, to Senor Usual?"

Rosa rolled her eyes. This wasn't the first time Bella had gotten on her about Pedro. "He didn't ask me anything. He never does."

Bella turned to her with her hands on her hips. "Yes, he did. He comes here all the time, and believe me; it's not for the flowers. He is hoping you will give him the time of day."

Rosa shook her head. "You know I don't have any time in my day. Taking care of Abuela Jacqui is almost a full-time job all by itself. Not to mention all my other full-time jobs."

Bella sighed. "There it is. I guess I will just have to be okay with my cousin eventually dying an old and lonely man. I should start introducing you to cats instead of men."

"I think I would prefer that. Cats are soft, loyal, and give you unconditional love, no matter what you do or how you look."

"Why would you be worried about looks? Any man would fall over himself to have you as his wife." She headed into the back of the shop and returned a few minutes later with an armful of roses. She began clipping off a small piece of the stem and then arranged them into vases and arrangements that she placed in a glass-fronted refrigerated unit next to the counter. "Then I guess you won't care who Rolando is picking up from the airport."

Rosa stopped what she was doing and looked at her. "That depends. Is it a cat?"

Bella watched her expression with interest as she said, "Arturo Espinoza."

Rosa nearly dropped the vase she was holding, barely catching it before it hit the floor.

"There it is. Now, you'll tell me that you don't care," Bella said knowingly.

Rosa hid her surprise and adopted a look of nonchalance. "Why would I care?"

"Maybe because you cried on my shoulder every day about handing him that rose by the lake? That's where your trust issues come from. Bella knows."

"And Bella is so humble, too," Rosa replied a bit sarcastically.

"Do you think he will come by and see you now that he's back?"

"Sure. He's probably thought of me every day since he left and is only back to take me away from all of this." She made a face. "You suck. You know?"

Bella walked Rosa toward the door. "Uh, oh. You're getting snippy. Here," she said, handing her a set of car keys. "You can get your mind off him by fixing my truck."

Rosa took the keys. "Sure, then I'll get all dolled up for my big date with Arturo."

Bella shrugged. "Who knows? Maybe you'll see him around. Now that you're all grown up, he may find you a lot more interesting."

"Geez, I hope nct."

Chapter Two

As the car rolled smoothly along, Arturo gazed out his window. After living in California's more temperate weather conditions for the past ten years, the oppressive heat of his homeland felt unbearable. He began to sweat. In the front seat, Rolando was oblivious to his friend's discomfort. He drove along, talking nonstop.

"Your dad is jazzed to have you back. It's all he talks about – not that he talks to me outside of giving orders, but he was pretty jazzed up when he told me to pick you up at the airport."

"Could you turn on the A/C, Rolando. I forgot how unbearably hot it gets down here."

"No problemo." He hit the controls, lowering all four windows. The wind and dust blasted Arturo, who fought to keep his hair in place.

"I said the air conditioning, not the windows!" Arturo yelled over the wind. Realizing that his words became lost in the wind, he gave up. "You know what? Never mind!"

Realizing that Arturo was trying to speak to him, Rolando pressed the buttons and closed the windows. "What did you say?"

"What's wrong with the A/C?"

"Oh, it's on the fritz. I can turn the fan on high. It might help a little."

"Figures," Arturo mumbled under his breath. As the hot air from the fan wafted back to him, Arturo wrinkled his nose.

"Oh, and sorry about the smell. I needed the car to get my kids to school this morning, and one of them poured the juice into the vents. I'm guessing apple."

Arturo surveyed the toys and stains splattered around the backseat like a kid-themed war zone. "Wow, kids. That's..." He sniffed and shook his head. "That's not apple juice." He looked up. "Are those footprints on the ceiling?"

"It's been crazy lately. You know how the farm gets right before harvest – twelve-hour days, driving around town whenever the call comes in. I barely get to see my children, and Bella is going full loco."

"Wait! Bella? Wasn't that the older girl with the..."

"Yep, she still has those. Hey, after work calms down, we should have you over. She's a terrible cook, but I could whip something up."

"That sounds amazing except...I'm not planning on staying long," Arturo told him.

"Oh yeah? How long?"

"I've accepted a position in a company in America. I start in a week. Coming back to work and sweating on a rose farm is not my idea of a career I want."

"Wow. I hope I'm not in the room when you tell your dad."

"Me, too." Arturo sighed.

"What's that?"

"I said I wish I didn't have to be in the room when I tell him, either."

Rolando shook his head. A moment later, he leaned forward to get a better look out the window at a truck in a parking lot that had a plume of smoke rising from it. "Uh, oh."

"What?" Arturo asked.

"That's where Bella works, and that's my truck smoking in the parking lot." He put on his turn signal to change lanes, which made Arturo uncomfortable.

"People are expecting me. Don't you think you should drop me off first?" he asked.

"No problemo. I promise to get you there right on time."

"Which in Colombia means…?"

"Absolutely nothing."

***

Beneath the truck, Rosa struggled to torque a wrench. "It's like…somebody tried to…," she strained mightily, trying to loosen a bolt. Something gave above her, leaking dark fluid onto her face, making her spit. "Blah. That got into my mouth!"

The sound of a car pulling up behind her on the left caught her attention. Peeking out, she watched as Rolando got out of a BMW. Then to her horror, she saw a face from her past. Arturo.

Oh no! No. No. No. Not now. She could not take her eyes off him. *Gah, he looks impressive.*

Arturo got out of the car and fanned his neck uncomfortably through his open shirt collar. "I think my hair is sweating," he complained. Ahead of him, he saw a pair of legs sticking out from under the truck. Somebody was hard at work.

Rolando, however, paid no attention. He was too busy fighting with his wife.

"What do you mean, what did I do to the truck?" Bella demanded.

"I'm just saying. It was fine yesterday, and you do have a history..."

"Is this about the squirrel again? It jumped in front of the car. If anything, I was the victim!"

"You weren't the one I had to take to the vet," Rolando protested.

"And again…who does that?" Bella looked over and saw her husband's passenger. "Hola! You must be Arturo. I'm Bella, Rolando's wife." She hurried over and hugged him warmly. He was quite a looker.

"So good to meet you," Arturo said through his discomfort.

"You, too! Even if it means you have to meet me in work clothes."

"You normally look better than this?" he asked, giving her an appreciative look. "Did Rolando win a bet?"

Bella grinned and flashed a look at her husband. "I like him, Buñuelo." Turning back to Arturo, she said, "He had a six-pack for about two years and took full advantage." She paused a moment when a brilliant idea hit her. "Hey! You should come for dinner tonight. Don't wear any clothes you don't want stained. I have a friend you should meet." She gave Rosa a gentle kick.

Mortified and still under the truck, Rosa kicked her back. She had no intention of coming out from beneath it. After all these years, she did not want his first sight of her to be like this.

Bella threw Arturo the keys. "I need a minute with mi esposo. Why don't you two finish up here?" She started moving away, avoiding Rosa's gloved hand, reaching for her leg.

Arturo stood there dumbly, not knowing what to do. Finally, he said, "Hey, guy under the car, can I help with anything down there?"

Rosa bit her lip but held out her gloved hand to shake his. "No, thanks," she said, keeping her voice as deep as she could.

"Okay…do you want me to try the engine?"

The gloved hand gave him a thumb's up, so he hopped into the truck and put the key into the ignition.

Chug. Chug. Vroooom!

"All right! Yeah!" Arturo said with a grin.

As the engine roared to life, it shot out a cloud of exhaust that quickly filled the air around Rosa. She started coughing.

Watching the smoke pour out from under the truck, Arturo said, "That looks bad. Can you breathe?"

Rosa tried to breathe through her shirt. When that didn't help, she held her breath and flashed him another thumbs up. She watched his feet, hoping they would move away, but they did not move. Her puffed-up cheeks started turning purple. Finally, Arturo hunkered down and rolled the creeper out from under the truck, revealing Rosa, her overalls covered in grease, and her eyes wide.

"Hey, man, you okay?" He asked.

"I..." She began coughing, and her breath came out in a puff of black smoke.

It was Arturo's time to look wide-eyed. "Good heavens. You're a woman!"

"I'm afraid so. Excuse me." She stumbled to her feet, scooped up her toolbox and creeper, and headed for the shop, hoping to escape, but he followed her.

"Can I give you a hand?"

"No, gracias," she said hurriedly.

"Then, do I owe you anything…?"

"Rosa."

"Rosa," he grinned. "It suits you."

"Gracias, and no, you don't owe me anything. Why would you? It's not your truck. Besides, I'm just helping out my cousin."

"Not many women would know how to fix a truck or a car for that matter. You must be very resourceful."

"I do whatever needs to be done. I prefer to rely on my abilities over someone else's."

Ah, an independent woman. I like that."

Rosa reached Abuela Jacqui, happily pruning the bushes, and set down her load. Arturo handed her a handkerchief, which she reluctantly accepted and used to wipe her face. He glanced up at the sign above the store that read, *Everyone, Needs a Rose.*

"Then let me buy you some flowers to say thanks. This place looks cute, even if the name is goofy," Arturo insisted.

"It okay. I work here," Rosa said.

"I love the name," Arturo said, immediately changing his original thought. "You work here, too?"

Rosa nodded.

When her face was finally recognizable, he smiled charmingly at the pretty lady starting to peek out from all the grime. Still, he did not make the connection between the little girl with the rose and the beautiful woman standing before him. He was about to continue his conversation when he was interrupted.

"Arturo! C'mon, gomelo. Time to go, if you want to get home on time."

Arturo waved at his friend, who was standing by the truck, looking a little impatient, but as he turned to say goodbye, he found Rosa gone. It was just him and Abuela Jacqui, who had moved from pruning the bushes to the doorway with a peaceful smile. Her granddaughter might not have picked up on Arturo's interest, but Jacqui had.

Chapter Three

Back in the car, Arturo's mind was a thousand miles away as he stared out of the green-tinted window. Rolando was back to talking again, but his words fell on deaf ears.

"…respect, you know what I mean? I'm not saying that we should go back to how things used to be, but just maybe they were onto something." When he didn't get a response, he glanced over his shoulder. "Hey, I saw you talking to Rosa. How'd that go?"

His question finally brought a response from Arturo. He turned away from the window to look at Rolando. "Who?"

"Rosa. Bella's cousin. The woman who just fixed the truck."

"Oh. Not really. She sort of ran off."

Rolando shrugged his shoulders. "Huh. Just like last time."

Arturo was in the process of turning back to the window but stopped. "What last time?"

"Don't you remember? She was the little girl who gave you the rose at the lake that day."

Arturo looked out the window as if he might be able to picture that little girl again. "Huh."

***

The BMW pulled up to a beautiful hacienda – a white mansion surrounded by a vast green plaza. Behind it, row after row of greenhouses spread out as far as the eye could see. Arturo exited the car and looked at his family home with something like dread. He had not wanted to come back here. His life was different now. He belonged to another culture, another lifestyle. He saw his life behind a desk, doing something far more interesting.

Rolando stood behind him, holding his bags. "Home sweet home?"

Before Arturo could reply, the front doors of the mansion opened dramatically, slamming against the wall of the house. Out walked Jorge Espinoza, a 45-year-old, salt and pepper haired version of Arturo. "Arturo! My boy is home at last. Bienvenidos!" Without slowing a step, Jorge strolled down the steps and opened his arms wide. He hugged his son, who remained stiff and unyielding. His father did not seem to notice.

"Hello, sir," his son replied woodenly.

If his father ever took the time to pay attention to someone else, he would have realized that something was not right. "I have been dreaming of this day for a long time." Jorge turned to Rolando. "Take the bags up to my son's old room, Roberto."

"It's Rolando. I have been your foreman for almost..."

"Don't forget to wipe your feet."

Rolando's words from earlier came back to Arturo. *Not that he talks to me outside of giving orders.* During the years he was gone, his father had not changed one iota.

Jorge turned back to his son. "This way! You need to see the whole operation. It has grown every year since you've been away. It's gonna take some time for you to get back into the swing of things again."

"Actually, I was hoping we could..."

Jorge wrapped his arm around Arturo, shoving him forward to march across the plaza. "Mateo!" he called out to a man who was standing in the shadow of the porch. "This is our Director of Operations. Watch out for this guy!"

Mateo Marquez, a man in his early thirties, joined them, running to catch up and follow along at their side. Small and skinny, he had red hair and a mustache, which made him look like a starving rooster. He shook Arturo's hand, limply. "I've heard so much about you..."

"Don't let him get started," Jorge interrupted. He did a lot of that as though no one had anything important to say, but him. "He will talk your ear off." He jabbed his son's chest with an index finger. "Mateo's my right-hand man. He ran the numbers while I waited for you to get back. He'll catch you up on all the figures so you can see the big picture and take the reins."

"Dad, I think we should talk somewhere private."

As usual, Jorge just ignored him and swept his hand to encompass the whole farm.

"As you can see, we're only a few weeks away from harvest. We've hired extra crews and extra shifts to keep everything on schedule. It's going to be our biggest harvest, ye..."

His voice trailed off, and he slowed to a stop as he watched a black limousine roll up the drive. Mateo got a panicked look on his face that made Arturo's brow wrinkle. He wondered what the significance of this vehicle could be. Judging by the foreman's expression, it could not be good.

"Sir, what do we...?" Mateo began. The man was practically wringing his hands.

"Let me handle this," Jorge told him.

The limousine pulled up next to them, and the driver exited to open the door for a large, severe-looking man in a suit. Perez stood a head taller than the three of them. He looked down as he wiped his nose with a handkerchief. "Jorge, I have been waiting for your call. I'm starting to think that you are avoiding me."

"Not at all, Senor Perez. I'll have some good news for you soon," Jorge replied.

"I doubt it." His voice was condescending.

"This is my son, Arturo. Arturo, this is our banker, Senor Perez."

Arturo held out his hand.

Perez ignored it and eyed him dismissively. "Have you told him how much you owe on this place?" he asked Jorge.

"He just got home."

"Two weeks, Jorge. No more deferrals, and don't make me come out here again. It's beneath me," Perez said nastily. When it came to what he considered underlings, he was even worse than Arturo's father. He allowed his words to hang in the air. Then, finally, he gestured to the driver to open the car door. Dropping into the limo with a complaining grunt, he blew his nose into his handkerchief as the door slammed shut, and the car pulled away.

"Right after your tour, we need to talk somewhere private," Jorge told Arturo.

***

Mateo led Jorge and Arturo past rows and rows of greenhouses full of colorful roses. He was the world's worst tour guide. "And here are some more flowers, but these are pink."

"Take a break, Mateo." The foreman clamped his mouth shut and looked down.

Jorge turned to his son. "You're probably wondering about that business with Perez, but it's nothing to worry about. We'll have the payment for him as soon as the harvest comes in, and we replace the trucks."

Arturo noticed Mateo wince at the mention of the trucks. The man clearly did not have a poker face. "Trucks? We saw one broken down on the way here. What's wrong with them?"

"Some of our trucks are no longer up to code. Don't worry. It's a minor setback, but that's where you come in," Jorge replied.

"Me?" Arturo looked at him astounded. "I don't know anything about fixing trucks."

"Not fix, my boy. We need to borrow some refrigerated trucks for the harvest. I happen to know that they have more than they need at one of the local rose farms, so just talk to the owner, Sofia Barboza. I'm sure you can charm her into helping us out this once..."

Mateo sputtered and tripped over his own feet when he heard the name, Sofia."

"...and get her to sign off. Should be a piece of cake for you."

"Why send me? Why not go yourself?" He glanced at Mateo, whose glasses suddenly needed cleaning. He did so with his tie.

"Because you are the future here. This is your chance to start acting like it." He winked at his son. "Plus, you two might hit it off."

"Listen, before you start making any plans about me and the farm, we need to talk."

"You're right. This is a lot to take in, and you have just arrived. We can make business deals later," Jorge agreed.

As soon as he finished speaking, the first drop of rain fell. Jorge frowned, and Mateo bristled like a cat.

"I need to get inside. Relax, my son. Walk through a greenhouse, get to know the lay of the land." The rain began to fall in earnest. "Mateo! Come!"

Arturo watched them go, but the rain started coming down even harder. He wanted out, too. He ducked into the closest greenhouse.

***

Arturo examined the room. It was filled with rows of carefully marked plants in all stages of growth, from dirt to sprouts to plants. There weren't any blossoms yet. Taking off his jacket, he shook the rain off and hung it on a stand to dry. Since he had no intention of going back out into the shower, unless it continued nonstop, he looked around. He did not remember this greenhouse. It wasn't here before he had left to go to college in America. Turning, he saw a wrinkled face attached to the body of an elderly woman. She was practically standing right on top of him.

"Yah!" He jerked back and threw his hands up in the air.

Abuela Jacqui pushed a heavy bag of seeds into his arms. "Hold this. I'm old."

He caught it with an oomph as she pushed past him to water a row of planters.

Arturo was incredulous. *The lady from the flower shop?*

"What are you doing here?"

"What are any of us doing here?" She asked.

"That's…surprisingly profound," he responded.

"Abuela Jacqui?" A voice called from around the corner.

Rosa came around the corner, but she stopped when she saw Arturo. Still sporting a ponytail and wearing work clothes, she held a clipboard and stood in a workshop area lined with tables that held a variety of blue flowers. On the wall hung a sign with a picture of a blue rose under the words, *Dream the Impossible.*

"And the other lady from the flower shop. Rosa, right? I almost didn't recognize you without the war paint."

"Charming," Rosa replied.

Unimpressed, she kept her distance and continued working. He approached her, setting the bag of seeds on the table opposite her.

"What are *you* doing here?" Arturo asked her.

"I work here."

"Do they know that you are both cheating on them at the other place?"

She ignored him and made a mark on her clipboard.

"You should answer. I *am* your boss, you know."

Rosa sighed in exasperation and looked up. "We are there in the mornings. Rolando lets me come in late and work late. I need to stay close to Abuela since she isn't...all there anymore." She rolled her eyes heavenward.

Both of them turned towards the elderly woman. They watched as Abuela Jacqui ate a rose petal. When she realized that they were watching, she turned away, eating the next one in secret.

"I hadn't noticed." He looked around. "This place looks like a lab. What are you, Frankensteining in here?"

"I'm testing rose cultivars for their potential hybridization with a local Isatis Tinctoria."

Arturo scratched his head. "You seem to be under the impression that I'm smarter than I really am. Since moving away, roses haven't been my thing."

"I am trying to invent blue roses," Rosa informed him. Under her stoicism, it was clear that she was very passionate about this.

"What? Seriously? Those are supposed to be impossible to create."

"Exactly, but I think I'm onto something. I haven't gotten a bud yet, but if I'm right..."

"Then I get to retire young," Arturo said, finishing her sentence.

"No! It's not about making money," Rosa protested.

"You're right. It's about making a *ton* of money. It's right out of a business school textbook: A product people have dreamed about for centuries, and you're the only one with the rights. It would make millions!"

"You can't!"

He was just teasing, but she was genuinely horrified.

Realizing that she has just yelled at her boss, she took a deep breath and got herself under control. "I mean, this is my little contribution to beauty in the world. I would like to have and enjoy them, even for a moment, before they are sold off to some heartless corporation."

"Sure," Arturo said in a soothing voice. "It's only fair after all the work you are putting into its creation."

Rosa suddenly turned to look all around. "Where's Abuela Jacqui?"

Chapter Four

After searching the greenhouse without finding her grandmother, Rosa ran outside and found Abuela Jacqui standing in the rain, holding Arturo's jacket over her head and smiling serenely.

"Sorry." Rosa pulled her grandmother out of the rain and grabbed the jacket. "She does this sometimes when it rains."

Arturo snatched it out of her hand. "Does she always do it with a $1500 jacket?" He looked at it bleakly. "You can't get these wet!"

Rosa was taken aback, and she stood there staring at him.

"Sorry about that," he apologized. "I just..."

"It's okay. We need to get back to work, and I'm sure you have better places to be," Rosa told him.

"Rosa, I..." His words trailed off because she and her grandmother had gone back inside the greenhouse. Staring at the door in frustration, he said, "Actually, I do have a meeting to go to – an important meeting."

***

Arturo sat at a table in a small, homey kitchen as three children screamed and ran past. Rolando ran after them as Bella cleaned off the table and began washing the dishes.

"Rolando wanted to make dinner, but he's a terrible cook, so I whipped something up."

"Everything tasted great. Thanks for having me," Arturo said. "You have a lovely home."

"Ugh, I wish. I haven't been able to take care of this place since..." She yelled to Rolando. "Buñuelo, how old is number two?"

"He's two!" Rolando shouted back.

"Four years now," she said as she washed and rinsed a plate.

"They seem to keep you busy."

"You have no idea," she said, placing the plate in the draining rack. "Rolando and I haven't done it in a month and a half."

Arturo spewed out a mouthful of iced coffee, but Bella did not notice as child number two pulled her sleeve, blood dripping from his nose like a faucet.

"I hab a dosebleed."

Bella swooped in with a wet paper towel, totally unfazed. Pinching his nose, she led him away towards the bathroom. "He gets these all the time." She made a motion like she was picking her nose and pointed down to her son before heading into the bathroom. Inside, child number three squealed and splashed.

Before the door closed, Rolando leaped out the doorway like a prisoner making a run for it. He hurried into the kitchen. "Arturo! I need to ask you a favor."

"What's up?"

"Bella's the sort of person who needs time all to herself, or else she goes crazy," Rolando began.

"Is she an introvert?"

"No, she's a female."

"Sounds kinda tough on her."

"And me, Arturo," said earnestly. He sat down in one of the chairs." Rough on me, cause when she doesn't get time to herself, there is no time for Rolando, either."

"So, I've heard." Arturo gave him a look of commiseration. "A month and a half?"

Rolando frowned. "It's like I'm married to Telemundo. Look, I watch the kids on Fridays, so she gets one evening to herself, but this Friday, I have to work..." He left the rest of the sentence hanging.

Arturo chuckled. "Aaaah, no." He shook his head no and held up his hands, palms out like a man trying to stop a freight train.

"Gomelo, it's a piece of cake! They'll be at a nature festival. They'll basically watch themselves."

The last thing Arturo wanted was to get stuck watching three young, unruly kids. Having none of his own, he didn't have the first idea of what to do. "I'm only here a week. I'm not sure..." He was interrupted by the ringing of his cell phone. Excusing himself, he walked over to the far corner of the room and tried to listen through the household noise. "Lex? Thanks for calling me back. What's that? Yeah, blue roses."

He listened for a moment. "Very promising."

A man's voice could be heard through the phone. Then Arturo said, "Call Bill and Jack. Find out how much market potential we're talking about, and I'll lock it up on this end."

He paused one final time, ending the call with, "I'll know more soon. Yeah, I can stay for a couple of weeks. You got it. Talk soon."

He disconnected and pocketed his cell as child number three ran past screaming. Rolando was chasing but stopped when he realized that Arturo was off the phone.

"Did I just hear correctly? You will be here for a couple of weeks?"

"Uh…yeah, they asked if I could help secure some trucks for the harve..."

Rolando's eyes lit up. "Good! See you Friday night," he said with a grin.

"No! Rolando!"

Child number three ran past again. This time he was naked from the waist down. Rolando took off after him. "Come back here! You can't run around like that."

Bella leaned out of the bathroom doorway. "Arturo, things are going to get worse here before they get better. Would you like a ride home?"

"No, thanks. I'll walk."

***

After the chaos at Rolando's house, it was a peaceful night, and Arturo sighed in relief as he walked alongside the lake that reflected the starry sky. Being an only child, he had never experienced the uproar going on at Rolando and Bella's house. He stopped and looked wistfully around. It was the same location where he had first met Rosa ten years ago. The incident rushed back into his mind with perfect clarity. Grabbing a tree limb, he ducked around another branch that hung over the water, enjoying the silence broken only by the songs of nighttime insects and frogs. He paused when something caught his attention. On a rock, he spotted a pile of clothing. Then he heard a splash.

Surprised, Arturo turned to look at the lake. Someone was swimming in the water – a dark shape leaving ripples in the reflected starlight. He watched transfixed. As the figure swam towards the middle of the lake, a set of shoulders emerged from the water. It was Rosa, and she was naked.

As he leaned forward to get a closer look, the tree limb he held onto broke, sending him into the water with a loud splash.

Rosa was submerged to her neck.

"Who's there?" She demanded.

Arturo recovered quickly and stood up, trying to look cool. "Hello there."

"Arturo? What are you doing here?"

"I was just coming to see the old place. I didn't know you would be here..."

She ducked lower in the water so that it came up to her chin.

"...swimming," he said, finishing his sentence.

"Well, I am, so that means you can go! Please!"

"Sure, but you know, I've had a hard time getting two words out of you." He sat down on a large rock, setting her clothes in his lap. "I'd be happy to give these back if you would answer five questions first."

Rosa pondered a moment. "You get two questions."

"Four questions it is. What did you mean that day when you said, 'I've wanted to give you this for a long time?'"

"I'll give you three." She paused to think about her answer. "I used to sneak out here to watch you guys swimming. I thought you were cute. That was before I realized that all men are skirt-chasing pigs."

Her answer surprised him so much that he ignored the last half of her comment. "You thought I was cute?"

"Yes. That's your second question."

Darn it! He thought. Still thinking about the fact that she thought he was cute, his other questions left his mind. "Did you think about me afterward?"

"Sometimes... What about you?"

"If you're asking questions now..." He shrugged. "That rose was pretty much the nicest gift anyone has ever given me. I always wondered who you were, and what would have happened if I had run after you."

Then you saw me again and didn't even recognize me."

"You were a child. You have grown up nicely since then."

Rosa, who had risen enough to show her neck again, ducked back down to chin level.

"That's not what I meant!" He took a deep breath to regain his composure. "Look, it turns out that I'll be here for a little while longer than I had originally thought. Would you like to join me for dinner sometime?"

"You're out of questions. Clothes, please."

"Okay. A deal's a deal." He held them out toward her.

She glared at him.

"Just kidding. Here." He took off his jacket and wrapped it around his head. Then he held the clothes out when she could reach them once she crossed the water. "Satisfied?" he said in a muffled voice.

She watched him carefully, suspicious that he might peek. When she was satisfied that he wouldn't, she swam to shore and got out of the water.

"It seems like a lot. Taking care of your Abuela while holding down two jobs. That's not a question, by the way, just an observation."

Her shadow passed over him. "A lot of people have it harder."

"I just think it's noble." He paused when he felt her take the clothing from him. "And if that blue rose thing turns out, that will set you up for life. No more working at a flower shop with a goofy name. Right?"

"It's *Everybody Needs a Rose,* and it belongs to my Abuela. What's wrong with the name?"

Arturo chuckled. "Just that nobody *needs* a rose. They're not exactly food, water, or shelter. Right?" She heard the crunch of footsteps moving away. "Rosa?"

He carefully lifted the jacket to peek. Rosa was dressed and walking away along the lakeside. He shook his head. *Same as before,* he thought. *At least she isn't running and crying this time.*

Chapter Five

The following morning, Jorge stormed up the hallway of the hacienda, Arturo, and then Mateo trailing closely behind.

"I think you're getting ahead of yourself," Jorge said.

"Not really," Arturo reasoned. "If you want me to take the reins, I need to know what's going on – our debts, our deals, and any R & D projects. You can't expect me to go into this blind."

"Of course not, but you have the rest of your life to run the show. Just take your time and settle in," Jorge said.

That's the one thing I can't do, Arturo thought. His father's unwillingness to speed up the process was frustrating, to say the least. "Can I at least meet with the foreman? Get the key personnel in one room and hear what they have to say?" he asked.

"No. You don't have to sit down with them right now." He waved his hand. "Mateo deals with the workers. It's for the best. Ah, here we are," Jorge said as he stopped in front of a door that led into the room he wanted his son to see. Turning to Arturo with a flourish, he grandly opened the door and waved him inside. "Your new office."

Arturo took two steps, stopped, and looked around. The room was a complete mess. Stacks of folders and miscellaneous files were piled high on the desk. The couch was covered with empty fast-food containers, and trash littered the floor around a wire wastebasket, filled to overflowing. A glamour shot of Mateo hung on the wall behind the desk.

"Mateo, you were supposed to have this room cleaned and ready!"

"No problem, sir. It will be done."

"That maybe, but I wanted it ready *before* my son arrived. Get it done this afternoon, or else."

"Yes, sir. Right away, sir. It's only temporary."

Arturo took out his handkerchief and wiped at Mateo's name, painted on the glass in the door. It was permanent. He frowned. His father placed a lot of faith in the man's abilities, but he wasn't so sure. From what he had seen thus far, Mateo's performance was less than exemplary. he knew that the sooner he took over the reins, the better.

Jorge turned to Arturo. "Anyway, on to the big news. I have everything set up, and Sofia is ready for your romantic evening."

At the sound of Sofia's name, Mateo once more froze like a frightened rabbit.

"What about the *business* meeting?" Arturo asked, impatiently. He was far more interested in assessing the state of affairs concerning the farm and making sure that the harvest was shipped out on time.

"You can talk about business. Make sure you get those trucks but get to know each other as well. See what happens!"

"A lot depends on this deal, dad. I'm not comfortable treating it like a date." The thought of his father trying to hook him up with a woman just because she had money left him cold. Arturo wanted nothing to do with an arranged marriage. Once he got things straightened out, and the deal secured with the blue roses, he was heading back to the U.S.

"Trust me. She's the right kind of woman for you. Pick her up at five." He turned toward the door. "Mateo!" Jorge marched out the door, heading toward his next destination.

Mateo held back long enough to say, "Word to the wise. Don't let Sofia get you alone if you ever want to be seen alive again." He rushed out after Jorge like a puppy, anxious to please his master.

Arturo considered his words and pulled out his cell. "Rolando! Hey, do you own a suit?"

***

That afternoon, Rolando was back in the driver's seat, wearing an unimpressive, wrinkled suit and a scowl. "You know this means that I have a whole day's work to make up. Right?"

"Yeah."

"You don't sound the least bit contrite about it."

"It can't be helped," Arturo told him. "A deal is won or lost in the first minute. I have to show up dressed to impress my driver. Then it establishes dominance and shows no weakness." He sniffed and wrinkled his nose. "What's that smell?"

"Cotton candy and vomit."

Arturo cracked the window and shot breath spray into the air. "You need to take better care of this car. How am I supposed to invite someone to ride with me with this foul smell, less alone the mess the kids leave in the back seat."

"Sorry, I'll try to keep it cleaner."

The journey continued until, eventually, they passed a gate that opened onto an enormous estate with sculpted hedges and a fabulous mansion that looked like a sprawling palace.

"You're not scared to be alone with her?"

"What?" Arturo looked away from the magnificent view and turned to his driver. "No," he scoffed. "Should I be?"

"Depends upon which rumor you believe. Me? I believe them all." He pulled the car up in front of the entry, parked it, and came around to open the door for Arturo. There was a long, stretching staircase that would bring them to the massive double doors. Guards stood on either side of them – armed and ready battle if needed. Their presence made both men nervous, and they exchanged glances.

"This is just a business deal," Arturo told Rolando in a quiet voice. "I eat and breathe meetings like this all the time. It's simple. The coolest head wins." He paused when he got close enough to get a good look at the doors. "Are those bullet holes?"

Rolando looked. "Oh, yeah."

Arturo put on a brave front, but inside, the feeling of uneasiness grew.

The door opened, revealing Sofia Barboza, wearing a black dress that fell just below the knees, and diamonds on her ears, neck, and wrists. Her legs were long and shapely. She was a perfect ten.

Arturo's jaw dropped. He hadn't been sure of what to expect, but it wasn't the picture of perfection that stood before him.

"How's your head?" Rolando whispered out of the side of his mouth. "Is it cool? Can I feel it?" He reached out to touch it, but Arturo slapped his hand away.

That evening, Arturo walked through an expensive restaurant complete with massive gold and crystal chandeliers, linen tablecloths, and exquisite paintings on the walls. The clientele consisted of the cream of society, yet every patron turned to stare at Sofia, who walked elegantly at his side. He couldn't help noticing that they all knew who she was, and they looked terrified. No one greeted her, and should she glanced their way, and they hurriedly lowered their gaze. When they finally arrived at their table, Arturo reached for her chair to pull it out, but she grabbed it out of his hands and pulled it out herself. His uneasiness grew as they sat down. He tried to look collected while she stared at him like a shark sizing up its next meal.

He cleared his throat. "So, Sofia, why don't you tell me a little about yourself."

"I don't think so."

Arturo mentally gulped but remained outwardly calm. "Straight to business, then?"

"No, small talk first. I've tried all the interesting men around here. Every one of them was a dismal failure, so when a handsome man drops in from America, I'm not letting him out of Colombia without a test drive."

An unpleasant shiver ran down his spine. *That was small talk?*

The waiter appeared, smiling fearfully at Sofia like she would eat him if he stopped long enough for her to grab him. "Good evening, Ms. Barbosa, what can..."

"We'll take two negronis, the belly appetizer – hot – and I want the fillet rare. Not medium rare, not half-cooked. *Rare*! Comprendes?"

"Yes, ma..."

"He'll have the vieira, so I can try that, too, and don't take all day."

The waiter did not answer. He was already gone.

"I hear that the vieiras are tremendous. I hope you're not allergic."

"Since that would kill me?" Arturo asked.

"Exactly."

"Nope." Arturo smiled. "You'll have to kill me some other way."

She threw him an intrigued smile and held up her hand. The waiter appeared instantly and placed a drink in her fingers. She drank it in one gulp without taking her eyes off Arturo. Then she handed the empty glass back to the waiter. Arturo's glass had been set down on the table. He reached for it, but Sofia snatched it away and drained it down in one gulp, too.

Okay then.

In the lobby, Rolando sat in one of the elegantly upholstered chairs, playing with his tie. Restless, he stood up and walked around the room until he came to a glass fish tank filled with lobsters that had fasteners around both claws, rendering them helpless and imprisoned.

Looking down at them, he said, "You and me both."

He wandered back to his chair.

Back at the table, Arturo's phone buzzed.

"Sorry. I forgot to turn that off," he said.

"Go ahead and get it," she said flatly. "I insist."

He nodded, pulled his cell out from his pocket, and answered in English. "Hi, Lex. You have the numbers?" He paused to listen. "Wow, that's a lot."

Sofia watched his every expression like she was just waiting for the right moment to attack.

Arturo tried not to react. "Don't get too excited. They haven't appeared yet, but it should happen soon." Glancing at Sofia, he gave her a smile, but he was too uncomfortable in her presence to keep his conversation going. "Actually, this isn't the best time. Let's talk later. Uh-huh. Yeah. Yeah. Okay. Bye."

He smiled as he punched off and pocketed his phone. She smiled back like she knew every one of his secrets.

"Before we get sidetracked, I'd like to nail one thing down. You have access to a fleet of trucks..."

"Your dinner," the waiter interrupted as he swooped in, followed by more servers carrying silver-covered dishes. They revealed the dishes contents with a flourish, then quickly set everything down on the table and disappeared faster than they had appeared.

"Ugh, finally," Sofia said.

She took a bite of steak that looked as though it had just been cut off a freshly butchered bull.

"Is that rare enough for you?" Arturo asked.

She moaned happily and smiled, revealing teeth that dripped red.

Horrified, Arturo looked away, reached for the appetizer, and took a bite. His eyes popped open wide, and his face turned red. Looking for his drink, he found only the empty glass where Sofia left it. Desperate, he signaled for the waiter, motioning for water, and grabbed a slice of bread from a basket that kept it warm. Biting off a big hunk, he chewed to help relieve the fire in his mouth until the water arrived, which he chugged down in relief. Sofia dicn't even notice.

"Okay, let's try this again," Arturo began. "We need trucks..."

"Hold on. I gotta tinkle."

Chapter Six

Rolando waited in the BMW while Arturo walked Sophia up the steps to her front door.

"...so, I told the priest, 'No, *you* go to hell,' and punched him in the throat."

"Witty," Arturo said, restraining the need to shiver. When they were halfway up the staircase and approaching the front door, he knew that he had to get this business with the trucks settled before she went inside. "Before you go, we never got the chance to talk business. It's vital."

"Okay, okay. Take your shot," Sophia said.

"With the harvest coming, our farm needs refrigerated trucks..." His sentence was interrupted when a German Death Metal ring tone sounded.

Sophia held up one finger. "Sorry, gotta take this." She answered her phone. "Si. No. Then you tell him that it is unacceptable!" She took a calming breath. "How unacceptable? It's I'll come to their house, kick open the door, and make their ancestors weep when they see what I do to their corpse unacceptable! You got that?"

Arturo leaned back. Hearing her words made him want to run away and forget the whole thing. Even if she did allow them the use of the trucks, he was afraid to think about what kind of payment she might want in return. And heaven forbid if he could not meet her demands.

"Uh, huh. Okay. Bye. Love you, too." She punched off her phone. "Sorry I have to go. What were we talking about?"

Arturo's chest was tight, and his throat constricted with terror. "Nothing."

Sophia shrugged and then leaned in and started making out with him like a female version of Don Juan seducing an innocent maiden. When she finished, she turned and disappeared through the front door of her home, saying, "Bye."

After the door was slammed in Arturo's face, he turned and slumped back to the car, where Rolando stood next to the car, trying to catch a bit of the breeze.

"How did it go?" He asked.

"I have no idea."

Rolando strolled back to the driver's side of the car, picking his teeth, leaving Arturo to get his own door. "At least the evening wasn't a total loss. The lobster was fantastic."

***

The following morning, Jorge walked into the dining room, as was his usual routine. He was barely inside the doorway when he spotted Arturo, lounging at the table, still wearing his clothes from the previous night, which he had slept in. A look of abject defeat was on his face.

Jorge decided to take that as a good sign and sat down across from his son. "How'd it go with Sofia last night?"

"I didn't get the trucks if that's what you're asking," Arturo replied. "By the way, I think she's certifiably insane and might actually be the devil, or maybe his mistress."

Jorge leaned in, his eyebrows raised. "But did the two of you hit it off?"

Arturo gave him a look of exasperation. "I don't get you, dad. I just told you that we missed our only chance to save the farm, and you want to know if I got lucky?"

"It's how business works down here. Trust me. There's nothing more important than getting you connected with the right people."

"The right people! Really? Dad, Sofia is a terrible person, and I am willing to bet that her so-called 'people' are just as bad," Arturo stated dramatically. He found himself becoming more troubled with his father's tunnel vision and single-mindedness. Arturo had even begun to wonder how the farm was still in business. Once Jorge had made his mind up on something, nothing seemed capable of changing it, no matter how wrong he was.

"My boy, you can't listen to rumors."

"Rumors? The waiter was late with the bill, and she threatened his children! On the drive back from the restaurant, she grabbed the steering wheel to make the car veer toward a family of ducks for heaven's sake. I believe those rumors are all too true – every last one of them."

"She is also from one of the oldest families in Columbia," Jorge added, as though that would make any difference at all.

"I hear you, dad, but I think you're missing some real opportunities with the people you've already got on your team."

"Uh-huh." Jorge took a bite of toast and chewed thoughtfully until his son's words penetrated his brain. "You mean the workers?" He asked with a frown.

"If you would only talk to them, I'm sure you would be surprised by what they..."

"No, son. Keep your distance. Trust me on this. You are better off with Sofia."

Arturo reached across the table to take his father's hand. "Dad, Sofia is *evil*. Your grandchildren would have horns and pointy tails. If we're lucky, we'll never see her again. Do you hear what I'm saying?"

Their conversation was interrupted by the blare of a horn. The sound drew them out of their chairs to the window, where they looked out to see a fleet of refrigerated trucks pulling up outside. The first one halted, and Sofia hopped out and waved to them.

Arturo was astounded. "Sofia?"

Jorge grabbed his son's shoulders and looked him in the eyes a moment before straightening Arturo's suit. "Looks like you did better than you thought! Now get out there and finish the deal." He grinned. "If you know what I mean." Jorge gave a thumbs-up and pushed him toward the door.

***

The workers gathered around the pristine trucks, impressed and relieved. The harvest would be saved, the money collected, and their jobs secure for another season. Rosa and Bella were all smiles as Rolando, and his crew patted each other on the back. Mateo was there, too, still as nervous as ever. As soon as he saw Sofia step out of the first truck, he backed up to hide behind the other workers.

The doors of the hacienda opened, and Arturo headed out to join the celebration. He and Rolando shared a nod.

"Well done," Rolando congratulated him with a wink. "Looks like things went better than you thought they did."

He was about to reply when Sofia caught him by surprise.

"Hello, Arturo."

He had not seen her approach, but suddenly she was there kissing him full on the mouth. The celebration paused as everyone watched in shock and horror, especially Rosa. Her expression was one of shock, and she walked away. The others might have followed her, but they were too afraid of Sofia to make such an obvious, daring move.

Arturo's words came out with a whoosh as the kiss was finished. "Woo, what?"

"This is an apology for cutting our date short last night. Let's find someplace where we can finish things right away," Sofia murmured. Her hands began to roam his body, much to Arturo's embarrassment.

He gulped. "Find someplace?"

"Bathroom, work shed, behind those bushes? I'm flexible."

"Oh, uh…good. Just give me a minute. Okay?"

"You have exactly sixty seconds," Sofia replied humorlessly. She was an impatient woman in everything she did, and this was no exception.

Arturo chuckled and ran to Rolando, pulling him behind one of the trucks.

"Hey, Arturo, you…gyaaa!"

"No time to explain, but I need to shake this woman," Arturo said quietly.

"Are you kidding? She just gifted us with a fleet of trucks. You can't tell her to take off! We need them to save the harvest."

"I know, I know, but she's gonna…she wants to..." Arturo allowed the panic show on his face.

Rolando shrugged. "Hey, that's not the worse anyone has ever had to do for the team."

"Are you kidding? She's a barracuda. I'll be lucky to come out of it alive."

Rolando raised an eyebrow, his expression one of disinterest.

"Look, I just need to shake her without it looking like that's what I'm doing." He looked pleadingly at his friend.

"All right. All right! Let me think." Precious moments passed, and then an idea popped into his head. "I have it!"

Then they heard Sofia's voice. "Time's up! Grrrrrrrowl!"

Arturo shivered in fear. Even if she wasn't the kind of woman she was, he had no interest in any kind of personal relationship with her or worse yet, her family. That road could easily lead to an early grave.

***

The door fell open as Arturo and Sofia tumbled inside the house with Sofia draped all over him.

"This your place?" She looked around distastefully, but she supposed it was still better than a bathroom or behind a bush. At this point, she would do anything to satisfy her urgent need.

"No. It belongs to a friend. I have something I want to show you," Arturo replied. On their way over, she hadn't been able to keep her hands off him, and he nearly wrecked the car. His hair was messy, and he had lipstick smears on his cheeks and lips.

"Sounds perfect, because..."

"Tio Arturo!"

Sofia froze in shock. "What was *that*?"

The sound of running feet approached as three children charged around the corner of the kitchen to jump on Arturo like a bunch of koala bears clinging to a tree.

"Hey, kids! Great to see you!" Arturo laughed.

One of the children looked up at Sofia. "Are you our new tia?"

The kids eyed her like a pack of coyotes ready to pounce.

"Arturo, what's going on?" Sofia took a step back as she tried to avoid direct contact.

"Sofia, these are mis sobrinos. Aren't they great? I can't wait for us to have some of our own."

"Some...sobrinos?" she stammered. She took another step back, a look of distaste on her face.

"Kids! Its what life is all about. How many are you thinking of having? Five? Nine?"

The middle child tugged on Sofia's sleeve, blood dripping from his nose like water from a faucet.

"What's...? Yaagh!" She retreated even further.

"I hab a dosebleed," the boy told her as though expecting her to do something about it.

Arturo swooped in with a wet paper towel, totally unfazed, pinching the boy's nose and leading him away. "He gets those all the time. I'll take care of this. You just watch the other two for a second."

Sofia staggered back, falling into a sofa chair. The youngest child ran past her pantless, waving his booty before running off. The more she saw, the more she wanted to get up and run. Then she turned her head to find the oldest child staring at her. She found it downright unsettling.

Arturo peeked around the bathroom door and had to bite his lip to keep from laughing. As he suspected, the mighty Sofia was being cowed by three small children.

"Shouldn't that one be wearing a diaper or something?" Sofia asked the oldest child.

"He was," came the reply.

"Where is it now?"

"You're sitting on it."

Sofia's eyes popped wide open in horror. When Arturo exited the bathroom, he found her marching away, wiping the back of her slacks with paper towels. He rushed to her side, a look of concern on his face.

"Sofia! What's wrong?"

"I'm leaving!"

"But…why?"

"This just isn't going to work out, Arturo. If somebody's going to be throwing a fit and screaming, I would prefer that someone be me. Call me …never."

Arturo followed her out the door, then slowed down and let her go. He watched as an expensive black car stopped next to her. The driver got out and opened the door for her, but she grabbed the keys from him, shoved him inside, and got behind the wheel. The tires squealed and spun as she raced away. Turning to Rolando and Bella, who had been hiding behind the bushes on their property, he gave them the thumbs-up. They grinned and returned the gesture.

Their victory smiles faded, however, when they heard a motor rev up from inside the house. Both parents ran inside.

Chapter Seven

Rosa slid into the new truck and slammed the door. She sat there, just breathing and rubbed her eyes. She could not believe what she had just witnessed. She felt surprised, sad, and angry, all at once. Her thoughts raced around her mind like a million neurons in a science project, until she finally drew a blank. After a moment, she picked up the microphone connected to the CB radio from the dashboard and set the channel. "Bella? Are you there?" She heard nothing but static. Her voice sounded impatient this time. "We're supposed to get these trucks moved. Where are you?"

The passenger door opened, and Rosa turned to see Arturo climbing inside.

"Hola."

"You've got guts. I'll give you that," Rosa said angrily.

"I was hoping to talk to you." When she said nothing, he continued. "Bella said that you needed a buddy to drive these anyway, so..." He trailed off, hoping to get past her anger long enough to explain.

Rosa stared straight ahead and started the engine. "Then shut the door. You're the boss."

As the truck bounced over rutted dirt roads, she stared ahead angrily.

"Any chance you're going to let me explain about Sofia?" Arturo asked after five minutes had passed.

"It was pretty clear – American businessman, Colombian businesswoman. Rich, beautiful, just your type. I'm sure you'll be very happy together for infinity."

"It was a business deal gone wrong. Actually, the business part went great," Arturo began.

She turned her head and glared at him, then turned back to continue driving.

"Just the business part! Sofia got the wrong idea, and I just broke it off with her," he continued. "I swear, Rosa. She is nothing like any kind of woman I would ever want. The whole time I was with her, I felt like shark bait, just waiting to be torn to shreds."

"Uh, huh."

"Seriously! Ask your cousin. I could be over there at their house with Sofia right now, but instead, I'm…I'm here with you."

Rosa continued driving, but the ice began to thaw. In her mind, she had a mental picture of what he was describing, and she bit her lip to keep from laughing out loud.

"Oh good, your eyes are drying." Arturo sighed with relief. "I gotta tell you, crying women are my kryptonite. The brain shuts down, game over." He glanced at her again before continuing. "I used to have a girlfriend who could fake it. I bought her two cars before I finally figured it out."

"Well, you're safe with me. I never learned how to fake crying," Rosa told him.

"It's terrifyingly easy. Just pull a nose hair. Here." He reached for her nose.

She slapped his hand, and they both laughed.

"Do you have any plans this weekend?" he asked.

Rosa shook her head in wonder. "You're persistent. I'll give you that."

"And cute, or so I've been told," he said with a grin.

Rosa glanced at him sideways. "You're not busy? I heard you were taking Bella and Rolando's kids to the Nature Festival tonight."

Arturo slapped his forehead with the heel of his hand. "Oh! I forgot all about that."

"Well, if you want time with me, you'll have to cancel. Won't you?" she said with a knowing look. Actually, she wanted to see what kind of person he was. His answer would help her decide on whether or not she was still interested in him.

"I can't. Sorry, but I promised Rolando. I wouldn't be much of a friend if I bailed on him at the last minute," Arturo explained.

"No, you wouldn't." She smiled. He had passed the test. "Okay. I'm in. Pick up the kids, and I will meet you there."

"Like a date?"

"Like apparently you have never watched three kids before. If somebody told you that it's a piece of cake, they lied."

Arturo was excited, relieved, and annoyed all at once. "Rolando!" he cursed under his breath. While he appreciated the opportunity to spend time with Rosa, he wasn't thrilled that instead of two, there would be five of them.

***

Rosa waited in front of a carnival-like row of tents in a park. She looked lovely in a comfortable yellow summer dress. Her hair lay soft about her shoulders. She smiled when she saw Arturo approach, struggling to hold the older kids' hands, while the youngest rode on his shoulders, hanging onto two fistfuls of his hair.

"Having fun yet?" She could not help teasing him.

He grimaced, hoping he would still have hair left by the time this night was over. "I could do this all day."

Smiling, she took pity on him and gently pried the youngest child's fists from Arturo's hair and scooped him into her arms. Then she took the middle child's hand, creating instant harmony.

"Bless you," Arturo sighed. He was so relieved that the look on his face was comical. "Hey, while I'm giving you things..." He handed her a small package, temporarily taking the middle child's hand back as they walked.

"You didn't have to get me anything!" She protested. She opened the box to find a golden bracelet. Rosa wasn't used to receiving presents, especially expensive ones, and certainly not when it wasn't for some special occasion or holiday.

"I got it from the nicest place in town - not exactly Saks Fifth Avenue, but I hope you like it."

"It's lovely. Thank you." She smiled politely, but it was apparent that she wasn't exactly excited. She put it on her wrist, fumbling embarrassingly with the little catch.

Seeing Arturo give her a gift, the eldest child wanted to emulate him. He spotted a patch of pretty flowers and disengaging his hand, he hurried over to retrieve one. "Tia Rosa, look what I found!" He exclaimed. He ran back to hand her the flower he had just picked.

She lit up naturally at the tiny blossom and hugged her nephew. "Oh, it's lovely! Thank you!"

Arturo looked on glumly. He had expected that kind of reaction when he had given her the bracelet.

***

The group moved past displays containing animals, birds, reptiles, and insects from around the world. Rosa was just as amazed as the kids. She and the middle child looked at an insect display, but she noticed Arturo looking at her instead.

"I've never loved anything as much as that one loves bugs," he told her.

"You don't know the half of it," Rosa said. "He started a collection in his bedroom for fun. Bella only found out when the eggs started hatching."

Arturo laughed. "I'm glad I wasn't there when that happened."

"Me, too."

"How about you? What does Rosa do for fun?" Arturo asked.

She thought for a moment. "I don't...not really. The only time I ever have to myself is after Abuela goes to bed." She looked around at the lights, the crowd, the laughter, and music, and smiled. "I haven't gotten out like this in..." She pondered the thought for a moment. "It's been a while," she said with a sigh.

"Then we should make the most of it."

She was about to reply when she heard someone call her name.

"Rosa?"

The couple looked around to see who it was and spotted a handsome man named Pedro approaching. Rosa greeted him with a kiss on the cheek. Arturo clenched his teeth to conceal his jealousy. He did not know who this man was, but clearly, he was the competition.

"I haven't seen you outside the shop in years," Pedro said. "Great running into you."

"Nice to see you, too," Rosa said.

Pedro glanced down at her wrist. "That's a nice bracelet. Funny, I don't recall ever seeing you wear jewelry before."

"This is Arturo, my boss," she said, skirting the subject. "We're watching Bella's kids to give her the night off. Arturo, this is Pedro. We went to school together, and now I see him in the shop every week like clockwork."

"Mucho gusto!" He reached out to warmly shake Arturo's hand.

Arturo smiled, but he was on the defensive. "Mucho gusto, Pedro. You're in the shop every week, huh?"

"Of course. Nobody grows prettier flowers than our Rosa. Spying a food stand, he added, "arepas de chocolo! Those still your favorite? I'll get you one."

"Pedro! You don't have to do that," Rosa said.

Seeing an opportunity, Arturo stepped in front of him at the food stand and dug out his wallet. "She's right, Pedro. Let me take care of it, and I'll get some for the kids while I'm at it." He handed over the cash and took the candy.

"Muchas Gracias, Tio Arturo," the kids all clamored as they received the chocolate.

Rosa nodded in appreciation.

Pedro just shrugged. He did not have to be a genius to see what was happening here.

"Pedro has always loved the outdoors," Rosa said after taking a bit of her treat. "He used to lead the class trips up into the mountains." She turned to Pedro. "Remember that?"

"Hey, don't bring that up again, Thorny!" Pedro said with a laugh.

"I love nature, too. Great to get outdoors like this," Arturo chimed in.

"Really, Arturo? I took you as more of a city guy," Rosa said, somewhat surprised.

"I *lived* in the city, but I was raised out here. I love all these plants and bugs and stuff," Arturo said. It was evident to everyone but him that he was trying too hard.

Just then, the middle child ran up with an excited smile on his face. "Look what I found!" He held up his arm to show a massive tarantula on his sleeve.

Rosa gasped. "Oh my gosh. Don't move!"

"Hold still, bud. Let me get that," Pedro said, stepping forward.

"It's okay. I'll get it," Arturo declared. He reached for it, but the tarantula reared back angrily.

"Maybe Pedro should do it," Rosa said cautiously. She knew he had done so before but wasn't at all sure about Arturo.

"I did this all the time when I was a kid," Arturo insisted. "You just have to pick them up right..."

He tried to pinch around its body, but it lunged upward to latch onto his finger. Arturo managed not to scream as he held up the hand with the tarantula.

The kids screamed. "Awesome!"

Rosa shot into action. Grabbing Arturo's wrist, she quickly led him over to a fountain and plunged his hand into the water. "Here, they let go underwater." She picked up the tarantula correctly around its body. "I'll find out where this little guy came from. You okay?"

On the verge of tears, Arturo grit his teeth. "It doesn't hurt."

Rosa headed off with the kids, leaving Pedro and Arturo alone.

"I hope you don't mind me saying, but you're a lucky man," Pedro said, admitting defeat.

"Clearly," Arturo said in a trembling voice.

"I'm serious. I'd have taken worse than that to get a date with Rosa. She's one in a million. She deserves to be happy."

"Yep. Anyway, you have a great night," Arturo said. "See you around."

Arturo left to follow Rosa and the kids, leaving Pedro alone.

***

Hearing a knock, Bella opened the door of her home. The oldest and middle child dashed inside, dragging Rosa with them, but leaving an exhausted Arturo carrying the youngest child, who was asleep in his arms. The hand with the spider bite was bandaged up.

"Hi, guys," Bella greeted them. "I hope you had fun. They apparently did."

"We survived," Rosa said with a laugh. "Let's call it a win."

Arturo tried to pass off the sleeping child to Bella, but she was too busy talking to Rosa and didn't see. "I cleaned two bathrooms and grouted the sink, so I'm on cloud nine."

"Glad to hear it. When does Rolando get home from work?" Arturo asked. He tried to hand over the child again but nearly dropped him when Bella turned to yell over her shoulder.

"Brush those teeth, then right to bed! I'll be checking for wet toothbrushes." She turned to Arturo. "Oh, Rolando isn't working tonight. He said you needed him for some last-minute delivery."

Arturo was startled by her words, but he quickly recovered. "Oh, yeah. That's what I meant."

Bella reached out to finally take the child from his arms. "I'll take it from here. You go and take care of my cousin, Rosa."

She headed back to the bedrooms, but Arturo did not move. He was thinking thoughts that disturbed him. He hoped his feelings were wrong.

***

Arturo and Rosa strolled along a moonlit path across the farm. He hadn't said a word since they left Bella and the kids.

"Is something wrong?" Rosa asked him.

He hesitated before speaking. "Did Rolando turn into a good man? Is he good to Bella?"

She thought it over. "When we were kids, Bella wanted to be a dancer. She danced all the time, even in church. You couldn't stop her. Later, she applied to dance school and was accepted, but when it came time to leave, she married Rolando instead. They had a baby ten months later. After that, she never talked about dancing anymore."

"She gave up her dreams for him? Was it worth it?"

"She found something else that made her happy." She smiled at the thought. "In a way, it's good that she doesn't dance anymore. Have you ever seen Rolando dance?"

"Or try to. He was all..." He imitated a few awkward dance steps, making Rosa laugh.

They walked in silence for a moment.

"What makes *you* happy?"

"Abuela Jacqui's smile. The look on people's faces when they are given roses that I have grown." She glanced up at him. "The first blue rose in the history of the world."

Arturo's heart caught. "You did it?"

"Not sure, but they have started to bud. I'll know any day now," she said excitedly.

"Then you're gonna want some alone time with them. Got it."

"Actually, I was hoping to share that moment with you. Right boss?"

"Sure," he replied guiltily.

***

When they finally reached Rosa's home, they climbed the steps of the porch. The light flicked on automatically above them.

"I guess we're here," Arturo said.

"I guess so." They stood there and looked at each other until Rosa said, "I should probably get inside and make sure Abuela Jacqui is okay. Wait here a second." She ducked inside.

Arturo walked along the porch, looking at the rose bushes on the side of the house.

"Um...Rosa?" He stared out at the garden to see Abuela Jacqui in the moonlight, jogging through the grass, totally naked. He raced after her.

A moment later, Rosa came back out of the house. "Arturo? I can't find Abuela Jacqui. Any idea... Oh, My Goodness!"

She spotted Arturo walking back towards the porch, gently guiding Abuela Jacqui, who was now wearing his jacket.

"Such a beautiful night, isn't it?" Jacqui exclaimed.

"Sure is, Abuela Jacqui. Hey, let's get something warm to drink."

Rosa rushed over to them, struggling to remain calm. "Abuela, you scared me! You can't go running off like that."

"Stop worrying, child. We call it living life." She smiled up at Arturo and patted his cheek. "He's such a nice boy. You should invite him in. I'll make some arequipe."

Rosa took over and walked her to the door, pausing to turn to Arturo. "Thank you."

"No problem. You gonna be okay?" Arturo asked.

"I don't know." She was seriously worried. "She's never done anything like this before."

"It's okay," Arturo said soothingly. "For tonight, just spend some time with her. Better to think in the morning when things are brighter. Right?"

"You're right." Rosa took a deep, shaky breath. "I should go."

They stood there a moment, neither one realizing that Jacqui had left them. Arturo stared into Rosa's eyes as he lifted a hand to cup her cheek and leaned in. He glanced sideways and stopped.

"Um, Arturo?" Rosa said in a voice that was soft and expectant.

"The side yard," he replied, straightening up.

Rosa turned to see that Abuela Jacqui had turned on the hose. She stood under it with his jacket over her head, smiling peacefully as the water washed over her.

"Oh, no! Your jacket!" Rosa exclaimed. She started to run for her grandmother, but Arturo reached and grabbed her hand, stopping her.

"You know…I think she needs it more right now." He looked at her and smiled. "Just take care of her." He kissed her cheek. "Good night, Rosa."

Moving down the porch steps, Arturo walked away in the darkness. As he continued walking through the trees, he pulled out his cell phone and punched in a familiar number.

"Lex, we gotta talk. Things have changed. Call when you get this and don't make any deals yet. Okay." He hesitated before continuing. "I'll see you soon, baby."

When he lowered the phone from his ear, it still showed the contact's name on the screen. It read: Alexandra.

Chapter Eight

The following morning, Bella, Rosa, and Jacqui stood at the front counter in the flower shop, arranging flowers.

"She didn't!" Bella turned to look at grandma in shock and bewilderment. "Abuela Jacqui, you're worse than the kids!"

"I apologize for nothing," Jacqui said calmly as she picked up the arrangement she had just finished and placed it in a display case.

Bella and Rosa exchanged looks. Rosa rolled her eyes. Abuela Jacqui still wore Arturo's jacket. She had been unwilling to give it up the night before except to hang it over the back of a chair in her bedroom to dry.

"It's probably for the best anyway," Rosa said, changing the subject.

Bella's hand froze on its way to adding a flower to the arrangement she was working on. She turned her head to look at Rosa. "What are you talking about?"

"C'mon, Bella. We're from totally different universes. Look at this." She held up her arm, showing off the golden lattice cut bangle bracelet.

"Ooo, that's gorgeous!"

"I know!" Rosa replied, clearly upset. "He got this just as a 'hello' for a first date. Before this, the most expensive give I've ever received from a guy was that Menudo t-shirt. How do I even act with a guy like this?" She looked at the bracelet once more before dropping her arm.

"Oh, stop. Arturo's crazy about you, and he should be. You're the bravest person I know."

"Then why do I spend every day with my grandmother, growing roses for other people and their romances?" Rosa asked exasperated.

"Because you are kind and gifted and devoted to her, but it's about time you took care of your *own* heart. That's what he wants. I guarantee it."

"And you know that how?" Rosa asked as she added a sprig of baby's breath to the arrangement she was working on.

"The jacket."

Rosa turned her head and stared at her blankly.

"Girl, you're clueless. You know why Abuela Jacqui does that with the jackets in the rain?"

"To sabotage my love life?" Rosa gave her a deadpan look.

"Family history," Bella replied.

"What?"

"Family history. When Abuela was just a girl, there was a boy in town who wanted to date her, but he had dreams, too. He had just purchased a brand-new suit and was going to the city to make his fortune. He took every penny he had with him."

"I know Abuelo did not work in the city, so what happened?"

"Abuela went to the bus station to see him off. She cried and begged him not to leave. He tried to console her, and nearly missed the bus. They ran to catch it, but just then, it began to pour rain. Rather than see her get drenched, he gave her his brand-new jacket." Bella smiled. This was her favorite part of the story. "He never got that job in the city, but Abuela knew cne thing. He loved her more than the rest of his dreams combined. I know it's been a few years since Abuelo passed away, but she still misses him. Now I think she just goes there – back to that memory sometimes."

Rosa looked over at Abuela Jacqui. She had stopped working to stare out the front window. "I should say something to him. Right?"

"If you feel the same way," Bella replied. "Yes."

"Has Rolando ever done anything like that for you?"

Bella flashed a brash smile, but there was a sudden sadness to it. Her task finished, she headed into the back room. "We can't all have fairy tale romances."

***

Rolando surveyed the new fleet of refrigerated trucks with his hands on his hips. At his side, Arturo looked gloomy after hearing some awful news. He couldn't help wondering if Sofia had done it, just to be mean.

"Sabotaged? How?" Arturo asked.

"Something in the gas tanks."

"Sugar?"

"Don't know yet," Rolando said.

"Oh, man. What's the damage?"

"Beats me. We need Rosa to see if it's just bad or bad-bad." He shook his head in disgust. "The harvest is tomorrow, and one thing is clear. Somebody is trying to destroy our farm. I'll get Rosa."

"That's okay. I can get her," Arturo said. He wanted to talk to her anyway.

Rolando grinned. *Sounds like somebody had a great time last night. You want to talk about it like girls do?"*

Arturo took a deep breath. "I don't know, ñero. Rosa isn't like anyone I've ever dated before."

"I don't know what that means."

"Neither do I. She wasn't born with money, but she is less worried about it than anyone I have ever met. She has had to work for everything, but she is happier working. She *cares* about people. Like really cares for people. How do I even measure up to a girl like that?"

"Don't overthink it, gomelo. The most important thing is to just go all in. Tell her everything you are thinking. It can go a long way, and in my case, it wouldn't take too long."

"Then, you tell Bella everything?"

"Of course!" Rolando blinked rapidly. He was a horrible liar, and Arturo couldn't help thinking about the lie his friend had told Bella last night.

Over Rolando's shoulder, Arturo saw a taxi drive up to the hacienda. The door opened, and a passenger stepped out.

"Are we expecting visitors?" Arturo asked.

"Not that I know of. Especially..." He squinted. "Not any leggy blondes. Ah, well. Whoever it is, she'll probably just talk to your dad."

Arturo's blood froze at the words, 'leggy blonde,' and he started for the hacienda at a run. "I'll see what's going on. You keep an eye on things here."

"Without your help? Oh, well, I'll certainly try."

Arturo was already running as fast as he could in his suit and polished shoes. He had not expected this particular blonde to suddenly show up on his doorstep. If it indeed was her, her arrival could spell disaster in so many ways.

***

Arturo neared the blonde at the front door just as the taxi driver finished unloading her bags. She was about to ring the doorbell, so he quickly pulled out his phone to make a call. To his horror, the blonde answered.

"Hey baby, you won't believe where I am right now!" She said.

Arturo took a breath and plastered on a smile. "Turn around."

Lexi Montagna spun around to find Arturo behind her. She screamed in joy, leaped into his arms, and gave him a huge kiss. "Churro! I was going to surprise you."

"Believe me. You have. What in the world are you doing in Columbia?"

"I had some news for you. Oh, and I have been practicing my Spanish. 'Soy mirando para mi cariño! That means my darling, but it's also a kind of beer." She turned to the taxi driver. "Be careful, the luggage is cumbersome. Um, equipajes muy peligro."

The taxi driver stared fearfully at her bags. Instead of telling him that her bags were heavy, she had told him that they were dangerous.

Arturo started to say something until he spotted Rosa walking up the driveway. "Soooo, great! Let's get inside."

He started through the door as quickly he could with Lexi still clinging to him, his phone in his hand. The taxi driver gingerly set the first suitcase down on the step, shielding his face like it might explode.

Arturo rushed inside the hacienda through the front lobby, and up the stairs to a landing with tile the color of terra cotta and dark wooden doors that led to his father's office and a bathroom on the right, Mateo's office, a closet, and another hallway on the left. "Did you get my call last night?" he asked Lexi.

"It must have come in while I was on the plane. Everything happened last minute. I was telling daddy how much I missed you, and he was so excited about the blue rose deal that he said I should just fly down here and say bienvenidos in person. Isn't that a funny expression? It means welcome, but also good windows."

They headed for the hallway, but Jorge's office door opened. Arturo panicked and pushed Lexi through the closest door across the hall.

"Maybe you should stop here for a minute, baby."

"But I..."

He slammed the door.

Lexi stood looking down at the toilet in a comfortable, half bath with blue painted walls and white fixtures. The décor was strictly masculine. She considered, and then shrugged and unbuckled her belt.

Getting his expression under control, Arturo watched Mateo as he emerged from Jorge's office.

As soon as Mateo spotted him, he said, "There you are. Did you hear about what happened to the new trucks? My blood pressure is in the 200s." He checked his pulse as Arturo gently grabbed his elbow to moved him away from the office towards a different door.

"I heard. We're getting Rosa to look into it."

"What if the engines are ruined?" Mateo whined. "The harvest starts tomorrow."

"Exactly, so there's a big priority that needs your focus right now." Arturo walked him through the doorway of Mateo's messy office.

"Sure. What do you need?"

Thinking on his feet, Arturo said, "Clean this place up."

"That's a big priority? This would take me the rest of the day..."

"Awesome." Arturo walked out of the office and slammed the door. He ran back to the bathroom door just as Lexi emerged. He grabbed her hand to pull her down the hallway.

"That was a good call, Churro. Airline food does *not* agree with me." She looked around, confused. "Shouldn't we get my bags?"

Back outside, the taxi driver cautiously set down the second bag. He was so nervous that sweat rolled down his face from his scalp. Suddenly, the suitcase toppled over, making him dive for cover behind a large rhododendron bush with a terrified scream.

Back upstairs, Arturo said, "Nah, they're fine. Let's find a comfy place to talk. This way."

At the end of the hallway, they reached a back door leading outside. He opened it to find Rosa standing there, her fist raised to knock.

"Arturo! I..."

Arturo closed the door once more in a panic.

"Who was that?" Lexi asked.

He opened the last remaining door and shoved Lexi inside. "One of the workers. Here, isn't this better? I'll be right back."

Inside the closet and under a single lightbulb, Lexi evaluated the rows of cleaning supplies tightly packed around her.

Back in the hallway, Arturo took a deep breath to open the back door. "Lexi, it's great to see you."

Rosa stood, blocking his escape path. "Did you just call me Lexi?"

"What? No! I said taxi. Didn't I see you over by the front door?" He tried to laugh casually but was unsuccessful.

"Your dad doesn't let the workers in the front door, and there's a taxi driver out there who is making me nervous." She made a motion with her finger. "I think he's a little loco."

Behind her, Arturo saw his dad walking up the path. He grabbed Rosa's hand and pulled her inside, slamming the door. "C'mon in! What brings you?" He dragged her briskly through the hallway.

"Well, I wanted to talk to you about us."

Arturo looked around nervously. "Absolutely."

"Arturo? You seem distracted."

"Me? What? I'm not. I don't...huh?"

He heard a door open behind him. No time! Still holding her hand, he hurried to the entrance of Jorge's office and escorted her inside.

"I need you to hear this before I lose the courage," Rosa began.

"Sorry, wait here a minute. Okay?"

"But I…"

The door slammed, cutting off her words. Arturo rushed to meet his father, who began marching down the hallway.

"Arturo, did I see you outside talking to one of the worker girls?"

"How could I? They're not allowed in the house."

"Good point," Jorge said nodding. "How did things go with Sofia?" He reached his office and grabbed the doorknob. Arturo panicked.

"Byaaah!!"

Jorge's hand froze on the doorknob. He turned to look at his son.

"Sofia…left me, dad." Arturo stammered. "I don't think we'll ever see her again."

"Oh, Arturo, I could talk to her."

"No!" He took a deep breath to calm down. "I just need some time to get over her. Could we take a long drive and talk?"

"Sure, son."

"Great! Better take a bathroom break before we go," Arturo said as he guided his father to the bathroom and shoved him inside.

"Whoa! Did something die in…?

His words were cut off when Arturo slammed the door.

In Jorge's office, Rosa looked at her reflection in the mirror on the door. "He's helpless against a crying woman. Okay. Here goes nothing." She tried to fake crying. "Oh, Arturooooo!"

Nope. Nothing. She glared at her reflection, determined. "Fine! Desperate times call for desperate measures." Rosa leaned toward the glass and tried to pull a nose hair.

In the hallway, Arturo hurried to the office and opened the door to find Rosa picking her nose. "What are you…?"

Her hands shot down to her sides. "Nothing!"

He shrugged. It wasn't his problem. He grasped her hand to pull her back into the hallway. "Rosa, there's something I need to tell you."

Her eyes lit up. "Yes?" she asked, hopefully.

"Somebody messed with the trucks. I need you to look at the engines to figure out what's wrong and get them ready to ship the harvest tomorrow. Rolando said he thought that some had been put in the gas tanks."

The hope died on her face. "Oh. Work. Yes, sir."

They reached the back door, and he opened it to walk her through.

"We can talk blue roses and anything else, once that's done. I promise. Okay?" Arturo asked her.

Rosa sighed and, in a resigned voice, said, "okay."

"Thanks for understanding."

Arturo went back inside and slammed the door to find Lexi standing on the other side.

"Did you say, rosas azules?"

Arturo jumped in surprise, dropping his phone. It landed unseen by his foot. He grabbed Lexi's hand and led her back downstairs towards the front door. "Uh, yeah! Pretty exciting, right? Now, let's get out of here, Rosa."

"Did you just call me Rosa?"

Arturo nearly bit his tongue. "Yeah, it's a…Columbian thing."

"Oh." Lexi smiled.

On the front porch, the taxi driver placed the very last bag with the others. Setting it down, he heaved a sigh of relief.

"Sorry, there's no room ready for you tonight, but there's a really nice hotel in town," Arturo said.

"If that's what you think is best," Lexi said, hesitantly.

"Absolutely. I'll come to see you tonight once you're checked in to your hotel and have had a chance to freshen up from your trip."

He grabbed her bags and literally tossed them back into the trunk of the taxi, making the driver cover his head and whimper. A moment later, Arturo waved as the cab drove away. As soon it was out of sight, he sprinted away.

Chapter Nine

A long, gravel-covered road stretched through the property, running past the rows of greenhouses. Parked along, it snaked the trucks that were supposed to be used to transport the harvest. Rosa was leaning under the hood of the closest vehicles when Arturo approached. She had already inspected the others. Although she was aware of his presence, she chose to ignore him for the moment.

"What have you found?" He asked anxiously.

"Sugar in the gas tanks."

"Is that...bad?"

"It's supposed to be," she replied. "Back in junior high, I heard that it was an easy way to jam up the works. The only way to fix it was to replace the engine."

Arturo's complexion paled. "Oh, man. That's not good – not good at all. We'll be ruined!"

"Of course, that was junior high." She paused on purpose, making him sweat a bit more. "The truth is, the filter catches most of it. We can replace those for, I don't know, maybe a couple hundred bucks?"

Surprised, Arturo gave a massive sigh of relief. "Then you're saying that whoever is sabotaging the farm is..."

"They're an idiot. Yep." She pulled out the old filter and tossed it in a pile, containing the ones from the other trucks.

"Can I help?"

"Sure," she said. "Hand me one of those filters."

Looking around, Arturo spotted stack with several boxes of filters piled together. He walked over to the stack, pulled one out, and removed it from its box. Then he took it over to Rosa and after handing it to her, held up the hood so that she could use both hands.

"Back at the house, what did you want to talk about?" Arturo asked.

Rosa shook her head. His timing was lousy. This was not the time or place to discuss personal issues. "Never mind. What about you? You were pretty worked up about something."

"Yeah, you could say that. A business partner of mine dropped by. Surprised me, actually. I wanted to talk about some potential market opportunities."

"Sounds complicated. Like what?" Rosa asked as she popped the new filter in place.

"Actually, I've meant to talk to you about..."

"Arturo!"

Arturo turned to see his father standing nearby, angry. "I thought I made myself clear when it comes to fraternizing with the workers, especially the women."

"Oh. I'm sorry," Rosa apologized, turning from the truck to face her employer. "I didn't mean to..."

"You're fired," Jorge said.

Stunned, Rosa clamped her mouth shut. A feeling of dread filled her. She needed this job. It was the only way she could support herself and Abuela Jacqui. The income from the flower shop would barely keep a roof over their heads.

"Dad, what are you doing? You can't do that to her!"

"Can't I? Get back to the house. *Now*!" Jorge shouted.

"She's fixing the trucks for tomorrow. Everyone depends on it, and she's the only one who can..."

"I said, *go*!" He grabbed Arturo by the collar, flames of rage practically shooting from his eyes.

The two men stared eyeball-to-eyeball, Arturo, now as angry as his father. He took a firm stance physically, and his hand formed a fist. It looked like they might come to blows – two bulls facing off. Which one would achieve dominance.

"Please!" Rosa grabbed Arturo's arm, pleadingly. "It's okay. Do as he says."

Arturo gave her a quick glance.

"Please," she begged, her tears trickled down her cheeks.

Jorge sneered at her before releasing Arturo's collar and storming off to the house.

"He can't do that, Rosa!"

"You know he can, Arturo. He's still the boss."

"That doesn't make it right!" he ground out.

"No. It doesn't, but Arturo, we're from different worlds, and unless or until you take over the farm, he will do as he pleases."

Calming down just a little, he looked at her sadly. "What will you do?"

"I'll finish the job. Like you said, everyone depends on it. Right?" She smiled but could not stop the tears from falling. "You should go. Please." She turned back to the truck and wiped her eyes with the sleeve of her shirt.

Arturo hesitated, looking from Rosa to Jorge. His chest felt tight from a combination of anger and compassion. Determined to have it out with his father, he stormed after him, catching up as Jorge reached the back door.

"How could you do that?"

Jorge turned to face his son. "I could ask you the same thing. Is *she* the reason you chased off Sofia?"

"No! I chased off Sofia because she is a conniving, cold-hearted, snake-in-the-grass, and I would never be able to trust her or feel comfortable with her. You have no excuse for treating Rosa like that. She is one of the hardest workers on the farm and totally devoted to it. Even though you fired her, she's back there busting her butt to fix those trucks, so that we can have a harvest tomorrow. Rosa is the one person keeping you out of bankruptcy!"

"And she smiles and tells you all the sweet things you want to hear, too. They're all the same," Jorge sneered.

"You've never even talked to her or any of them for that matter. To you, they're little more than slaves, paid to do all the hard work and come running at your call, just like Mateo does. He's nothing more than your lap dog, and it's sad and sick to watch. How could you possibly know anything about the workers?"

Jorge had turned his back on his son to go inside. Instead, he swung around and snarled, "Because your mother was one!"

Arturo stepped back, stunned. "Mom?"

"Our family always had money," Jorge fumed. "I had no idea how good we had it. When I grew older, I became interested in your mother. Your grandparents tried to warn me. They told me what would happen if I married beneath me. I didn't listen. I thought it didn't matter. I thought I knew better." He calmed a bit and sighed. "It was like somebody had turned off the lights. I wasn't wanted or invited to the places I used to go. Business partners stopped calling me back. Every single day just got harder than it needed to be. Then, Perez took over the bank, and he has been trying to kick us off this land ever since."

"Why? What difference does it make as long as he gets his money?"

"I don't know. Maybe he thinks it would prove his point. As far as he is concerned, when I married your mother, I was soiled, ruined, no longer part of the so-called upper class."

"Do you regret marrying mom?"

Jorge didn't know how to reply to that. Did he regret marrying the love of his life? Maybe not. He had loved her, and when she died, he felt like the gentler side of himself died with her. He became a hard and bitter man. Did he regret ruining his family's business because of it? Yes. He once had hoped that with her death, things would return to normal. It didn't happen. As far as the powers that be were concerned, he was tainted. Not only him but his son as well.

He wasn't about to share any of that with Arturo. Instead, he said, "I just know that it made life harder, and if you're honest with yourself about whats-her-name, you would realize that you don't belong with her. Back in America, were you looking at the cheerleaders or the cleaning crew?"

"That's hardly a fair comparison…"

Whatever else he might have said was lost as Jorge walked through the back door, leaving Arturo to think.

***

Jorge walked inside and heard a buzzing coming from the floor. He reached down and picked up Arturo's phone, reading the name on the screen: Alexandra.

Still, inside the taxi, Lexi held the phone as it rang while speaking to the driver.

"Perdóname, take the exit to the city, please. Um... Éxito en la cuidad."

The driver tossed her a look over his shoulder.

Lexi's screen popped to an image on the other end. It was Jorge.

"Hi, Arturo, when did you say you were coming to..." Her words ground to a halt when she looked down and realized that the image on her screen wasn't Arturo. "Oh, hello."

Jorge smiled. "Hello."

***

Arturo rang the bell in the quiet, luxurious lobby of the eight-story hotel and waited for someone to come out to the desk. Marble flooring in various shades of brown and cream led to a large mahogany check-in desk, centered against the back wall. There were three stations with computers, ready to serve the hotel's guests. Massive round columns divided the room on each side, leading off to various lounging areas, each with a sizeable, expensive rug and comfortable stuffed furniture.

"Can I help you, sir," the concierge asked from her station at the center of the desk.

"Yeah, I'm looking for a guest here, Alexandra Montagna. She checked in a little while ago."

The concierge checked the computer. "I'm sorry, sir. I don't see anyone by that name. Are you certain she checked in?"

"Actually, I lost my phone somewhere. She should have arrived before now. I sent her over in a taxi quite a while ago. You're sure she isn't here?"

She rechecked her screen. "Quite certain, sir."

Puzzled, Arturo left the hotel and walked outside, making his way up the sidewalk. *I wonder where she is?* He thought. *I hope she isn't doing something I'll regret.* He glanced across the street and was about to move on, but what he saw brought him to a screeching halt. Through a window, he saw dancers moving to the music inside the studio. One of them was Rolando. He was dancing with a beautiful dancer, who definitely wasn't Bella. Rolando said something, and his partner smiled and held him tighter. Arturo continued to stare, totally stunned. Was this where Rolando had been the night he had told Bella that he was doing a job for him?

***

Later in the early evening, after returning from the city, Arturo knocked on Rosa's door. He wanted to talk to her. She seemed so clear-headed and smart that he hoped she could help him come up with a way to convince his father to rehire her. After hearing about his mother, he wasn't sure that was possible, but he had to try. He stood waiting, and when he didn't hear anyone approach the door, he tried again.

"Rosa? Are you home? Abuela Jacqui? Please answer the door."

No answer. Still, he hesitated. Where were they? When it was clear that no one was home, he stepped off the porch and left.

***

Arturo walked under the stars on a path between the greenhouses, hunched over and agitated. The trucks had all been repaired and were waiting for the next day. Then, they would be loaded with this year's harvest and sent on their way. Now in the darkness, they loomed like sleeping giants, waiting to awake with the morning sun.

His world felt like it was falling apart around him. He was still reeling over the news that his mother had been a worker. He wanted to hear the rest of the story, but trying to get it out of his stubborn father would be worse than pulling teeth. Now Lexi was missing. What had happened to her? Why hadn't she gone to the hotel like he had told her to do? If anything happened to her... He tried to stop thinking. It was just too much. Looking up, he spotted someone on the path ahead of him.

"Abuela Jacqui?" He called as he hurried to catch up with her, and then adjusted his stride to match the elderly woman's leisurely pace. Glancing at her face, he saw that she wore her usual peaceful smile and carried a potted rose plant. It was a sad example without any buds or blooms. The plant reminded him of Charlie Brown's Christmas tree. "Rosa wouldn't be happy with you, wandering around the farm by yourself."

"She's not the boss of me. I'm working."

"Is that why you're taking some poor plant before it's had a chance to get dressed up?" He asked.

"Shows what you know," she said condescendingly.

They walked together a while longer until they heard Rosa's concerned voice in the distance.

"Abuela Jacqui!"

"I've got her," Arturo called, relieved to hear the sound of her voice. "Over here."

A moment later, Rosa ran up the path, breathing heavily. She looked at her grandmother. "What are you doing?"

"Special delivery."

"Who would order a plant without any...?"

"Bah." Not deigning to answer, Jacqui pushed past and kept going. Rosa and Arturo fell in step on either side of her.

"You can't just take off like that, Abuela Jacqui. I was so worried," Rosa said.

"Stop worrying. It'll make you old before your time," Jacqui told her.

"I won't be able to take care of her if she starts doing this," Rosa told Arturo. She paused before continuing. "Not that I could take care of her anyway without this job."

"I'll talk to dad. He overreacted. I'm sure that once the harvest is over, he'll cool down." He turned his head to look at her. "There is going to be a harvest. Right?"

"I finished the trucks. Some of the guys are watching them so that I could come to find Abuela. Apparently, just in time."

Music wafted through the air, and they slowed together.

"You hear something?" Arturo asked.

"That's the harvest celebration. We have it...the workers have it the night before. It's a tradition."

"Do you think that's where she was?"

Arturo looked ahead. Abuela Jacqui had never slowed and was now well ahead of them. They rushed to catch up.

Chapter Ten

The work location, a large red barn that had been cleared and decorated with wildflowers and streamers, was alive with light, music, laughter, and dancing. Using a loading platform as a stage, a band blared out lively cumbia music on guitars, trumpet, and percussion, while several workers sang their hearts out to the heavy beat. The barn doors had been thrown open wide, and people were gathered both inside and out. Abuela Jacqui wandered inside with Arturo and Rosa trailing behind her.

"Looks like the whole farm is here," Arturo shouted to be heard.

"That's the idea!" Rosa told him.

Scanning the room, Arturo spied the workers and their families colorfully dressed, dancing together, and eating from a wide variety of food piled on tables that were lined up along each wall. The place was filled with laughter and warmth – like a picture from home, and Arturo felt a pang of bittersweet memories of when he was very young. His mother had brought him to the festival that year before she died. His father never went, but his mother was so beloved by the workers. He had forgotten about it and what it was like back then, thanks to his father's strict upbringing and insistence that he could not socialize with the workers.

Bella approached and hugged her cousin. "Rosa! So good to see you guys."

"You, too!" Rosa said. "Where's Rolando?"

"Running another delivery into town." She tossed Arturo a dirty look. "Not that he could dance a step anyway, poor man." She glanced around as she spoke. "He said he would be here... Oh! There he is."

Rolando made his way through the surrounding throng, smiling and out of breath. "Hola, everybody! Sorry, I'm late." To his surprise, Abuela Jacqui handed him the potted plant.

"Rolando? Why did she just give you that poor rose plant?" Bella asked.

"I called the store earlier to order some roses…for you, cariño. I ordered "El Especial." He looked at the sickly plant. "I was expecting something a little more special."

"Hurts when people aren't honest, huh?" Arturo said, giving his friend a meaningful look.

Rolando was surprised to see the accusation in Arturo's eyes, but Bella interrupted the moment to kiss her husband on the cheek and accept the plant. "Well, if that's what Abuela Jacqui picked out, it must be special. Gracias, Buñuelo. I know right where we'll plant it."

"Okay, Abuela, we should head home," Rosa said. She looked uncomfortable and anxious to leave.

"Nuh-uh. We finally got you out to a fiesta, and I'm not letting you go so easily," Bella told Rosa as she moved up next to Abuela. "I have her. You go dance out there. You, too," she said Arturo.

Almost on cue, a new song started up, but Arturo ignored the music. "Rolando, I need to talk to you," he said. During the conversation between the others, he had not taken his eyes off his friend.

"We can talk later, my friend. You need to focus," Rolando replied. He didn't know what Arturo's problem was, but this was an excellent opportunity to push him and Rosa together, and he wasn't going to let it pass.

"I'm serious. This is important!" Arturo insisted.

Suddenly, he found himself pushed up against Rosa. They were face-to-face, the music was swelling, and she was stunning.

"So is this," Rolando whispered. "Try to keep a cool head, Arturo."

Rosa and Arturo stumbled into the middle of the mass, everyone moving in rhythm. The couple started to sway, his hands on her hips.

"Whoever made these shoes, I don't think they had dancing in mind," Arturo said.

Rosa looked around nervously. "I shouldn't be here. Your father has already fired me. Can you imagine what he would do if he saw us like this? He would go ballistic."

"Then it's a good thing he never comes to a worker dance," Arturo said with a smile.

"What if people talk? I don't want to make trouble. I mean, Abuela..."

Arturo lifted her chin and looked into her eyes. "Maybe Abuela was right. We should stop worrying."

Arturo pulled off his shoes and tossed them against a wall. Then he loosened his tie and held up his hands. Rosa stepped up to place her hand in his. They faced each other, and his right hand slid to the small of her back. It was an electrifying moment.

"I don't know the steps," Rosa said softly.

"We'll figure them out together."

The music picked up, and they began to move – a little awkward at first. Then Arturo started to get into it, and they plunged into the fray, dancing faster as the music sped up. The scene was vibrant and warm, with smiling couples young and old. In the middle of it, Rosa danced with Arturo in his socks.

The steps were fast, but they moved in harmony together as the band played faster and faster, ending in a mad rush. Rosa stepped away from Arturo with a flourish, allowing him to take a bow. Everyone laughed and applauded. The workers, most of whom were hired after Arturo's mother has passed, had never had a boss party with them before.

Arturo grabbed Rosa's hand and led her off the floor.

"That was fun!" She sighed, hating what she had to say next. "But, I need to go."

"What? You have more work to do for free?" Arturo teased.

"If today is my last day, I want to go by the greenhouse one last time," she said.

"Then, I will go with you."

"I couldn't ask you to do that." Rosa's brow wrinkled slightly to match the concerned look on her face.

"You'd better. Otherwise, you would be trespassing." He wiggled his eyebrows up and down. "We frown on that."

Rosa giggled. "I guess you had better come then."

"If you insist."

She smiled.

***

Inside, the greenhouse was quiet and dark until they turned on the overhead lights. The rose beds were neat and orderly and seemed to stretch on forever. Rosa, however, was interested in only one section – the one where she was trying to grow a new species of rose. She moved from station to station, tenderly feeling the leaves of each plant. Behind her, Arturo carefully showered a bed of rose sprouts with the contents of a watering can.

"Careful! Not too much," Rosa warned.

"You sure you want me to do this for you?" He asked. "I still don't know that much about growing roses, and I would hate to mess things up."

"One step at a time. That's how we learn."

He watered the next bed, careful to get the amount just right. "Right. Get the rules down."

"Sort of," Rosa said. "It's not just science. There's an art to growing roses. You have to watch them closely and give them what they need, along with a little tenderness every day."

"You ever work that hard on a plant, just to have it turn out bad?" he asked.

"Sure, but usually, it wasn't the plant's fault," Rosa assured him. "It was mine. I'd get impatient, try to force it to do more than it could instead of loving it for what it was."

"Loving it?" Arturo asked, puzzled.

"That's the secret to growing roses, Arturo."

"I'm starting to get it." He thought a moment before saying, "*Everybody Needs a Rose*. It's like…" He had been looking ahead to the next bed and froze in place.

"You're not going to make fun of the store again. Are you? It's really not as funny as…"

"Rosa."

"I mean, really, Arturo…"

"Rosa!"

Concerned, she moved to his side to find him staring intensely at one of the rose plants in the next bed, so she leaned closer and saw…a single blue rose.

She dropped her clipboard, and her hands flew to her mouth. "I don't believe it." She reached out with trembling fingers to stroke a tender petal.

"You did it," Arturo said in a hushed voice.

Her eyes met his. "I did it?"

"You did it!"

She took a deep breath and then screamed. Arturo picked her up and swung her around in a circle, both of them laughing.

"Just wait till we tell da..."

He never got to finish his sentence. She kissed him passionately, and the world held its breath as the kiss went on and on. He kissed her back, the fingers of his hand-woven into the hair on the back of her head.

Rosa stepped back, still looking deeply into his eyes. "We…we have a lot to celebrate."

"Then, let's celebrate. I have a bottle of wine at the hacienda," Arturo said.

"Workers aren't allowed in the hacienda," Rosa reminded him.

"Then, it's a good thing you aren't a worker any longer." He smiled charmingly and took her hand.

The couple ran up to the house and entered the foyer.

Rosa looked around nervously. "Are you sure this is okay?" she whispered.

"Of course. If it makes you feel any better, wait here for a minute." He rounded the corner into the kitchen and straight to the fridge. Opening it, he grabbed the bottle of wine.

"A bottle of wine! Excellent! I was thinking the same thing," Jorge said.

Arturo jumped in surprise. Turning, he saw his father at the dining room table sitting across from Lexi.

Chapter Eleven

"We've got a lot to celebrate. Don't we?" Jorge asked his son. The smug look on his face said it all. He had him right where he wanted him.

Arturo was stunned. He looked back and forth from his father to Lexi to Rosa, standing behind a corner where they could not see her.

"I was on the way to the hotel when your dad called me. He found a room for me here, after all." She held up her fist in triumph. "Yay!"

"Imagine my joy when I discovered that my son had such a lovely American girlfriend."

Arturo glanced at Rosa. His heart seemed to restrict when he saw the hurt expression on her face.

"Gracias," Lexi said shyly. "You Columbians are such charmers."

"She was just telling me about the blue roses," Jorge said. "Why don't you tell him, too?"

"Lex, wait!" Arturo said.

"Why? That's what I came down here to tell you. You were right. As soon as we told them we could grow blue roses, we had investors lining up. We just needed a signature on the paperwork."

Jorge held up a contract and a pen, beaming. "Now they have it! I sent Mateo to get your files together. We're officially in the blue rose business." He took the bottle of wine from the stunned Arturo and popped the cork.

Lexi clapped. Arturo turned to run out the door, but Jorge grabbed his arm. He switched to Spanish. "Where are you going? This is everything we have ever wanted."

"Everything *you* ever wanted, dad, but then you have never believed that there is anything more to life than money. Have you?" He tore himself out of his father's grip and ran out the door.

At the table, Lexi held two glasses of wine, confused. "Sorry, I didn't catch all the Espanol."

"It's fine. I'll go get him. You get started without us," Jorge told her.

He went after Arturo, leaving Lexi alone. She held up one of the glasses of wine. "To blue roses." She drank half of it down.

***

As Arturo ran past a row of buildings, lost in thought, something caught his eye. Up ahead behind one of the greenhouses, he saw smoke. As he rounded the corner, he discovered a dark figure kneeling to set fire to the building.

"Hey!"

The figure jumped to his feet and ran away. Arturo raced after him. Up ahead, the shadow leaped over a fence but tripped. Landing hard, he was forced to limp away.

"I have you now! Arturo shouted as he reached the fence. With one foot on the top, he was about to clear it when he heard his father's shout.

"Fire! Get help. There's a fire!"

Arturo glanced over his shoulder and stopped cold. The greenhouse was in flames. He glanced at the fleeing figure once more, but he had no choice. The fire had to be stopped. Jumping down, he ran back toward the greenhouse where his father stared blankly at the wall of flame.

"What do we do?" Jorge asked.

Arturo had never seen his father appear so helpless. He spied a garden hose attached to the side of the building and ran to turn it on. Water gushed out for a few seconds, but then it stopped. He tested the nozzle again, but the water had been turned off. Throwing down the hose, he looked at his father. They stared at each other helplessly. Whoever had started the fire had also made sure they couldn't put it out easily.

"Arturo! This way!" Rolando shouted.

Rolando and the other workers appeared out of the darkness, carrying buckets from the next greenhouse over. The workers began to pour water on the flames while others hosed down the other buildings to keep the fire from spreading. Arturo and Jorge ran to grab more buckets, as they joined the workers in aid.

The smoke Arturo had spotted earlier was coming from another greenhouse further away. It quickly raged out of control. Flames from the two buildings shot high into the air as fire shot up their wooden frames, burning them like matchsticks. Windows exploded, showering everything with shards of glass, and the wind picked up the burning ash and debris. They just couldn't keep up with it.

"Arturo, where are the blue roses?" Jorge asked.

Seeing how far the fire had spread, it hit Arturo. "Rosa!" He took off, racing for the greenhouse that held the new roses, fearing that he would find her there.

"Come back!" Jorge shouted. "It's too dangerous!"

***

Her greenhouse was already on fire when he arrived.

"Rosa!"

Instead of an answer, all he could hear was the roar of the fire and the explosion of windows. Running for the door, he jerked it open. Heat and smoke from inside blasted him off his feet. Arturo scrambled to his feet, soaked his jacket at the outside faucet, and covered his head. He charged inside, trying to look through the smoke and flames for Rosa.

It was hell.

Choking, he stumbled through the smoke, shielding himself from the flames licking hungrily at the walls inside. It was almost too intense. Arturo fell to his knees, trying to breathe in the fresher air near the ground. In the commotion, he stumbled upon the unconscious Rosa. He didn't waste his breath calling out to her. He could see that she was unconscious. Picking her up and tossing her body over his shoulder, he headed for the exit. He had barely gone more than a few feet when the area between him and the door collapsed, blocking his path. Desperately, he looked in every direction. At the opposite end, the workshop area that was lined with blue flowers was the only place not burning. There, in the outside wall, the windows were still intact.

Setting Rosa down, Arturo wrapped his jacket around his head and shoulder and charged the windows, smashing the glass. Then he ran back to Rosa, lifted her once more, and ran through the opening, sheer willpower taking them a safe distance. Once they were safe, he set her down and collapsed at her side. Catching his breath and shaking intensely, Arturo got to his knees next to her and checked her pulse. He lifted her chin and began mouth-to-mouth until she began to cough and gasp for air. He held her as she recovered.

When she was stable, their eyes locked, breath heaving, with smoke-streaked faces close together.

"The…roses..." Rosa gasped.

Arturo leaned back to look at the greenhouse, but it was now completely engulfed. They watched helplessly as the blue roses, and most of the harvest burned in front of their eyes. A sense of utter loss and hopelessness engulfed them both. Without the money to rebuild, the farm would be unable to recover, and the workers would be out of jobs, their livelihoods as devastated as the greenhouses.

***

No one got any sleep that night. The greenhouses were gone – nothing but smoking piles of rubble remained. The workers, who had worked all through the night, continued pouring water on the hot spots. Rolando led them in their efforts, calmly directing the others. They knew what this meant; still, they continued on. What else could they do?

Jorge walked through the rubble until he stumbled upon something sticking out at an angle that hadn't been burned completely. He pulled it out. It was the sign from Rosa's greenhouse that read: *Dream the Impossible*. It was burned and scarred, the blue rose half blackened. Lifting his gaze from the sign he still held, he looked at the workers around him. They all looked the same – blackened clothes and faces streaked with tears. Rolando walked among them, comforting others but clearly crying himself.

Finally, he saw Arturo and Rosa sitting not far from the remains of the greenhouse that had held the precious blue roses. They stared at the devastation, her head resting against his chest. Jorge watched them until he noticed a limousine approach and come to a screeching stop. The driver emerged to open the passenger door for the imposing Perez. What had brought him here this morning? It was as though he had known about the fire and come to gloat, but how? Obviously, someone had told him, but who?

Jorge moved toward him, and Arturo rose to join his father, leaving Rosa still staring blankly at the destruction. Together father and son faced Perez in his prim suit, wiping his nose with a handkerchief.

"What a pity, Jorge. Just when things were looking so promising," Perez said. His voice showed no concern or sympathy. A smug smile was on his face.

Behind him, a smaller man scooted out from the limo to join him, walking with a noticeable limp. It was Mateo, and the truth of what had happened hit Arturo like a baseball bat.

"It was you, Mateo. You set the fire," Arturo accused him.

"Prove it," Mateo said weakly.

"How'd you get that limp?" Arturo shot back. "Hurt your leg when you jumped the fence last night. Didn't you?"

Still leaning on Arturo, Jorge stared at his former right-hand man. "Mateo? How could you?"

Mateo puffed up with righteous anger. "I'll do you one better. How can you ask *me* that?" Making a farce impression of Jorge, he said, "Hey, Mateo, do the heavy lifting on the farm for years so that I can hand it over to my son when he's done partying in America." His face lit up with an idea. "Better yet, find somebody who *appreciates* people who work for him!"

"Shut up, Mateo," Perez warned.

Mateo shriveled up. "Yes, sir."

Perez marched past them to look over the destruction. "Not much chance of making your payments now, Jorge. I'll have the foreclosure papers drawn up right away for you to sign. No sense in delaying the inevitable. Is there?" He wiped his nose. "I'll be back tomorrow. Then I will own this place, and I will be here a lot more." He smiled smugly, then turned back to his car. Mateo followed right behind him. The driver opened Perez's door and closed it; Mateo opened his own door. They drove off.

It was the last straw. Jorge broke down, collapsing against his son. Arturo let him cry. Rolando approached, concerned, to place his hand on Jorge's shoulder. Arturo turned and saw that Rosa was gone.

"Can you get my father back to the house," Arturo asked his friend.

"Of course. This way, sir," Rolando replied.

"It's…Rolando, isn't it?" Jorge asked weakly.

"Yes, sir. I've got you." Rolando reached out to support the older man, and the two of them started back toward the house, the only remaining, undamaged structure on the property.

Arturo watched them go and then took off running. He knew exactly where to find Rosa.

***

Rosa stood on the bank, her bare feet in the water as she looked across the lake. When Arturo found her, he stepped into the water, expensive shoes and all to stand next to her, but she did not move.

"Until a few weeks ago, I had my life all planned out. I was only supposed to be here long enough to say goodbye. Then it was back to America, Lexi, and that whole life." He paused for emphasis. "A lot has changed in the last few weeks."

"When were you planning to tell me about her?" Rosa asked woodenly.

"Technically, I *did* tell you about her."

"Don't you *dare*!" She flared up but then began to cry.

Arturo's heart ached. "I'm sorry. I should have told you everything, but I didn't expect all this to happen. Lexi flying down here out of the blue, the roses…it all happened so fast."

"Sure. You barely had time to tell me that you already had a girlfriend, and oh, by the way, I sold her your roses." Her throat caught. "How *could* you?"

"It wasn't supposed to be like that." He reached for her hand, but she stepped away.

"It's funny. I was starting to think we could be something. That you would have the guts to turn down the American dream, but you don't even have the guts, to be honest with me."

"You should talk," Arturo said defensively.

She turned and glared at him. "What's that supposed to mean?"

"You're gonna lecture me about guts when you have been holed up in your little store for the last decade?"

"You think I had a choice?"

"Don't give me that! Handing out flowers for everybody else. *Everybody Needs a Rose*, but the nicest guy in the world, Pedro, comes by to see you every week, and you run away – too scared to live your own life, just like you did right here so long ago."

"I quit!" Rosa shouted. She stared defiantly at him. Then thinking about it, she added, "I know. I'm already fired, and everything was burned down, but even if it wasn't, I want you to know that I am choosing this. I'm quitting. It's time for me to let go."

"What about Abuela Jacqui?" Arturo asked softly.

Rosa wiped her tears with the back of her hand. "We'll have to close the store. She will have to let go, too, but at least she will have the chance to say goodbye to *her* dream."

"Rosa."

She started walking away but paused long enough to look at him over her shoulder. "Goodbye, Arturo. Go back to America where you belong."

Chapter Twelve

Arturo walked along the shore, shaking his shoes as he tried to get the water out. Hearing a noise, he looked up and was surprised to see someone coming up the path towards him. It was Lexi.

"Hey," she said.

"Hey."

"I'm so sorry about the farm. Those two men should be arrested for arson and sent to prison for a long time."

Arturo sighed. "Yes, they should, but Perez is too powerful. No one is going to make him pay for his misdeeds."

She reached out and took his hand. "Let's find somewhere to sit and talk."

They found a beautiful shady spot under a wide-trunked tree and sat with their backs against it, looking out at the green trees and grass, a refreshing break from the devastation of the farm.

"You love her. Don't you?" Lexi asked.

"Truth is," Arturo began, "I have never felt like this for anybody. Now that she's gone, I don't know what I'm going to do with the rest of my life."

"Looks like you've had a busy couple of weeks."

Arturo smiled in spite of himself. "I didn't want to hurt you, Lexi, but I am done with half-truths. I don't want to hurt anyone I care about like that ever again."

"Then, I guess I owe you the same. Honestly, Arturo, you're the best man I know and given a chance, I believe I could have married you and been happy. What I don't know is if my love could ever grow enough to match the love you have for Rosa or hers for you."

"I was expecting something with a bit more sting to it," he admitted.

"It's true, though. Look, my dad owns a hedge fund worth millions, and I'm what…at least an eight. Right?"

"At least," he agreed.

"Then you can imagine that I have had other guys express an interest. Some of them were better looking, a lot had more money. I'm with you because you are the sort of man who would tell the truth to a girl like me. If love is really about working through life together, whatever comes, then you're the kind of man I would want to love me." She leaned in and gave him a peck on the cheek, then she stood up.

He joined her.

"There's no reason for me to stay any longer, so I'm gonna buy a ticket home for later today. If you're still interested in seeing where things go, I can make it two." Her eyes held hope, but she knew it wasn't meant to be.

He looked at her with genuine respect. "You're pretty special, Lexi."

"You, too, Churro."

He opened his mouth to speak but hesitated a moment. Finally, he said, "If we're honest, I've always hated that nickname."

She grinned impishly. "I know."

He reacted in surprise and then laughed. She laughed with him.

***

Abuela Jacqui moved about the store, as usual, humming with a peaceful smile on her face. She did not notice Rosa staring at the *Going Out of Business* sign she had just made through red, puffy eyes, nor Bella trying to comfort her.

"I'm an idiot," Rosa said.

"For what? For falling for a guy who screwed up? That's not idiocy. That's love, and you're not the first person to have this happen to you. It's all part of the game of life."

"If this is what you have been pushing all these years, I think I'll take the cats," Rosa said with a sigh. "Their love is unconditional and lasts a lifetime."

"Hey, heartache is part of the deal. A week doesn't go by where I don't want to throw Rolando out a window, but I know the big dummy loves me. It's like growing roses. You gotta deal with the thorns if you want to enjoy the beauty and fragrance of the blooms," Bella explained.

"Nice. Except I just lost my roses, too. If there's ever been a time to pack up and quit, it's now." She placed the *Going Out of Business* sign in the window.

From the corner, Abuela piped up without pausing in her work. "I don't see what you're complaining about. You grew blue roses once. Doing it again should be easy."

"Easy? It's all burned up, Abuela. All the research, all the roses it took painstaking years to create, working seven days a week to make sure they came out just right. Even if I could do it all over again, there's no guarantee that it will ever work. Even the plants I created them from are gone. It's no use."

Abuela Jacqui finally stopped and looked at Rosa. "If flowers are such a pain, what makes you think that love is easy?"

Rosa was speechless.

"Whoa! Point for Abuela," Bella said, using her index finger to draw an invisible one in the air.

"Then what should I do? Chase after him? Forgive him? Work it out with a guy who tried to sell my childhood dreams for a corner office and a life of luxury?" Rosa was flabbergasted.

"Don't be so dramatic," Abuela Jacqui told her. "Everybody messes up. Love means that you have to be willing to work through the messes together and grow closer instead of growing apart. All it takes is two people who want it more than anything else."

"What if we try and, in the end, we grow apart anyway?" Rosa asked softly. "Is it really worth all the suffering and pain it would cause?"

"Look at me, my dear," Abuela Jacqui said. "I am a million years old. I know everything comes to an end, and I miss your Abuelo every day, but I wouldn't give up those years we had together, just because they wouldn't last forever. Without him, my life would have been dull, filled with nothing but work and longing. I wouldn't have the treasured memories or the years of happiness he gave me."

"You didn't start growing blue roses because it was going to be easy," Bella added. "Have a little hope and see what springs up."

The door opened, and Pedro walked in. Bella gave Rosa a look that said, "See what I mean?"

"Pedro? This isn't your usual day," Rosa said by way of a greeting.

"I saw the sign," he said concerned. "Is everyone okay?"

"I'd say we're pretty far from okay," Rosa admitted. "We're gonna have to close down, and depending on where I find work, we might be moving, too."

"That's awful," Pedro said. The last thing he wanted was for Rosa to move away. "Is there anything I can do to help?"

"No, but it's lovely of you to ask," Rosa said with a brief smile.

Pedro paused, working up the courage, but Rosa beat him to it. "I could use a friend, though. Care to join me for dinner tonight?"

Pedro smiled warmly. Behind him, Bella and Abuela Jacqui high fived.

***

Jorge sat behind his mahogany desk, looking out the large windows at his once splendid view of the farm. Now it was nothing more than the burned-out husks of his greenhouses. The workers had wanted to clear it all way before they left, but he had told them no. "Let Perez do it. After all, he's the one who burned them down."

In his left hand, he held an old framed photo of himself, his young son, and the boy's mother. His heart was heavy, and he took a drink from the glass of wine he held in his other hand. When Arturo entered the room, he raised his glass. "Hey, Arturo! Have a drink." He downed the rest of the wine and set it down slowly, almost breaking it. "Perez won't be here for another hour or two. Let's live it up."

Arturo approached to sit on the edge of the big desk near his dad's chair. The office was in disarray, something he had never seen before as his father had always been organized. Papers were scattered about on the desk and floor. A bronze paperweight that looked like a rose in full bloom, a small wooden box that held pens, pencils, and a letter opener. There was a gold nameplate attached to a solid walnut block, as well as other objects that had shared space on the desk were scattered across the room, obviously thrown there in a fit of rage. Now the anger was gone. Only failure and lost hope remained.

"Quite a future, I laid out for you. The grand plan lasted…what? Nearly two whole weeks?" Jorge tried to take another drink but realized that his glass was empty, so he poured himself another from the bottle, his hand wrapped around the goblet as it rested on the desk. "That girl, Rosa. Where is she now?"

"She's gone," Arturo replied woodenly. "I failed, as well." Sliding the drink away from his father's hand, he lifted it and drained it all at once. Setting the empty goblet down, he looked at his dad. His heart also was heavy. Not only because he had lost Rosa, but because his father had lost his dream of a fantastic future for himself and his son.

"I want you to know something," Jorge began. "I loved your mother. No matter what anyone else says, I was never sorry that I married her. Not once. After she died…I only wanted what was best for you."

"I know, dad." Arturo placed his hand on his father's shoulder. "What happens now?"

"Perez is gonna take everything he can, but when it's all said and done, there's a patch of land he cannot touch. It's not much, but it might be enough to keep a small operation running. Enough for a father and son to handle, if you're up to it," Jorge suggested hopefully. He looked up at Arturo.

"Actually, that's what I came to talk to you about. Lexi told me that the job is still open for me in America. Do you think I should take it?"

"You want to know what **I** think? Since when?" Jorge asked, looking Arturo in the eye.

"A lot is changing."

"Then let me keep it going, son. I like Lexi, and you're not going to find a better deal than that. She can offer you a bright future. I no longer can."

"I know," Arturo admitted.

"What matters the most is doing what's going to make you happy. I can't make that decision for you. All I can do is be on your side, wherever you go, whatever you decide. I figure it's about time I started doing that."

Arturo began to tear up. "Thanks, dad. I appreciate that more than you could ever know."

They looked out the window together for a long moment.

"Seriously, though, we only have the wine cellar for another hour. Let's get cracking," Jorge said.

***

Standing on Rolando's front lawn, Arturo handed a crate full of wine bottles to him.

"More to pack. Thanks," Rolando said. He added it to an already significant pile of boxes. "I put in a call to a buddy of mine the next town over. There's a job ready for me, so all we have to do is uproot our entire lives in a weekend, find another place to live, and hope that Bella can find work somewhere as well. How about you?"

"The farm is getting foreclosed any minute now, so I'm thinking about going back to America with Lexi. She's taking the next flight out."

"Is that the blonde?"

"Yeah."

Rolando raised an eyebrow and whistled. "Did you tell her that you've spent the last few weeks chasing Rosa?"

"Yeah."

"Wow, man, I hope your job is in sales, cause you could make a killing at it."

"Look, I ruined everything with Rosa by not being upfront and honest with her." He stabbed a finger at Rolando's chest. "I would hate to see the same thing happen to you."

His friend looked puzzled, totally clueless as to what Arturo was talking about. "Absolutely."

Arturo waited for Rolando to confess, but his friend just smiled. "Rolando! I was in town yesterday. I saw you at the dance studio."

"Oh. You saw that?" Although surprised, his friend did not seem distressed about the discovery.

"Yes, and I want to know when you're going to talk to Bella about it."

"Relax, of course, I'll tell her. I'm just looking for the right moment. I want the mood to be just right."

"Huh?" Now it was Arturo's turn to be confused. "I'm not sure you should worry about the mood so much as..."

"Don't worry, gomelo. I have this. In all the years I have been married, I have learned one thing."

"Sounds about right," Arturo said sarcastically.

Rolando ignored him. "Love is all about commitment. That means that whatever else happens, I know we're going to face it together. Bella's not going anywhere, and neither am I. Even when she's old, wrinkled, and stuff isn't…you know, where it's supposed to be, she'll still be my one and only."

"Maybe you should write this down before you talk to Bella," Arturo suggested. "She might buy it."

"And you, man. You need to figure out who you wanna stick with for the long haul. If it's Rosa, you need to tell her. Don't give up so easily."

"Rosa's already gone."

"Could you ever love Lexi like that? Be a real man and learn from all of this? If so, get on the plane and go for it. You hear me?"

"Yes. I do." Arturo nodded and looked over to the house, did a double-take, and took a step back in shock. "Rolando. That rose plant Abuela Jacqui gave you at the dance. What happened to it?"

"That poor thing? I planted it over by the..." He turned to point at the house, where the rose plant grew under a window. The plant seemed to like its new home as it was blooming. The blossom was a blue rose.

"What time is it?" Arturo asked, unable to keep the excitement, fear, and hope from his voice.

A moment later, his BMW peeled out of the driveway.

***

Arturo drove like a madman, leaning forward intensely. In his hand was the blue rose.

The airport was a hectic scene, a sea of people that parted, revealing a woman checking in her bags. It was Lexi.

Arturo roared over the Columbian roads, passing cars, and pushing the pedal to the floor. "C'mon, c'mon!" He shouted. Adrenalin sang through his veins on overdrive. Weaving through traffic, he had a couple near-misses, causing other drivers to curse and shake their fists at him. He was blind to it all. Only one thing filled his mind. He had to get to the airport before it was too late.

Lexi wove through the crowd, her carry-on over her shoulder. She was sad to be returning home empty-handed. She had lost her dream, too, but she knew that she would rise above it and in the end, find something...someone else. She still had an hour before she needed to be at the gate and decided to take a walk. As she approached the airport doors, she stepped back, turning towards the street and looking to see if anyone had shown up to join her. At first, she saw no one, until a BMW screeched to a stop at the curb, and Arturo leaped out of the car.

As Lexi continued to scan the street, she turned in the direction of the car, and her face lit up. She waved.

***

Rosa smiled and handed a bouquet to a customer. "Thanks for remembering, *Everyone Needs a Rose!*"

The store was packed. Locals and workers filled the space, walking past the *Going out of Business* sign to purchase their last roses before the store was closed forever. Bella worked almost as hard as Rosa. The two women raised their voices to be heard over the warm chatter and kind words going out to Abuela Jacqui, who was hugging a long line of old friends that had come to support her. It was a bittersweet situation.

Lending an extra helping hand was Pedro. He worked behind the counter, wearing an apron, and exchanging a smile with Rosa. The door opened, and everyone turned to see who the new customer was. They stepped back as they recognized Arturo walking through the door and through the crowd. His expression was one of hope and expectance.

"Gracias! Thanks for remembering…," Rosa began.

The store suddenly went silent as she looked up, saw him, and froze.

Arturo stood in the middle of the store, catching his breath, reaching out to her, and holding in his hand the world's only blue rose. Rosa just stared at it. She had thought they were all gone until this moment, and she could not hold back the tears that streamed down her face.

"It's the plant Abuela Jacqui brought to the dance," Arturo told her as he approached the front of the counter where she stood.

Rosa looked at Abuela Jacqui through tear-filled eyes.

"You didn't ask," Jacqui said with a shrug.

Rosa wanted to yell at her and hug her at the same time.

"I saw it growing there at Rolando's house, and I didn't think about market shares or some corner office in America. I thought of you and the way your face kinda scrunches up when you get embarrassed." He smiled and pointed to her face. "There it is." He smiled hopefully.

Rosa looked at the crowd, nearly overwhelmed with emotion.

"And I realized, even if I got everything else I ever thought I wanted, it wouldn't mean anything if you weren't there to share it with me. If I have to choose between you and the rest of the world...I choose you." He stepped forward holding out the rose, offering it to her. "I know I messed up, but can you...?"

"Stop." Rosa took a deep breath and looked at Abuela Jacqui, Bella, and Pedro, who stood beside her, sadness in his eyes.

Then he smiled and said, "It's okay."

Rosa turned back and looked at Arturo, taking the rose in her hand. "For as long as I can remember, all I've ever wanted was you."

He pulled her close, leaning over the counter to finally kiss her. She wrapped her arms around his neck, the blue rose rested against his cheek. The crowd cheered around them as the couple looked deeply into each other's eyes and kissed once more.

"Hey, you two, get a room," Abuela Jacqui teased.

Chapter Thirteen

The gates flew open in the courtyard, which the hacienda had been built around. Perez strutted in like he already owned the place. Mateo trailed behind him, taking notes.

"...pave the whole thing. It's all way too green." He looked around at the flowers and bushes, still barking orders. "I want all this ripped out. Put a fountain here in the middle, something tasteful with a Greek statue. You know the kind that has naked ladies."

"Naked...ladies," Mateo repeated, writing it down.

As they proceeded, they found Jorge blocking their path, his arms folded.

"Ah, there he is. Mateo, papers," Perez said, snapping his fingers.

Mateo scuttled forward to hand a short stack of forms to Jorge. Jorge, however, did not take them. Instead, he continued staring hard at Perez.

"Oh, come now, Jorge. Today's the day. Face the music," Perez said. When he received no response, his eyes hardened.

From behind, Jorge, Arturo, and Rosa stepped up to join him. Rosa held the blue rose for all to see.

Perez's brow darkened, and he darted a fuming glare at Mateo but quickly collected himself.

"That's some flower, but unless you can turn that into enough cash to pay off the entire loan, it doesn't change a thing," Perez said.

"You're right," Jorge agreed. "I can't ...but she can." He pointed back toward the hacienda.

Behind him and out of breath, Rolando opened a door and held it open for Lexi, who held up a check in front of Perez's dumbstruck face.

"Get off our farm," Jorge growled. "And don't ever trespass on my land again." He looked at Mateo. "As for you, there's someone law enforcement people who want to talk to you."

Furious, Perez's face turned three shades of red. A moment later, he stormed out of the plaza, yelling and snapping at Mateo, who followed along, hoping that his new employer would be willing to keep him out of prison. Behind them, the others celebrated. Rosa gave Lexi a hug, and Jorge shook Arturo's hand.

***

It was mid-afternoon when Jorge took the stage to a gathering of cheers. The workers had all returned and built a platform on the grass for a massive fiesta. Everyone was dressed in their finest. Jorge stood behind a microphone located in front of a large display covered by a sheet.

"Gracias! It's wonderful to be here with all of you again. I want to thank each and every one of you for your hard work and loyalty. This marks a new day for all of us, and a new chapter in beauty for the whole world. Next year will be the first time in history that true blue roses will be available for sale, and the only place they will be grown is right here!"

The crowd burst into applause. Everyone was there. In front stood Rosa and Arturo with Abuela Jacqui, Rolando with Bella and the kids, even Lexi and Pedro, looking adorable together.

"We have had discussions with the team about what to name the blue roses. I'm happy to say that we're ready to make an announcement. To do the honors, let me introduce their creator and our new director of operations, Rosa Gonzalez!"

The crowd once more cheered and applauded as Arturo gently urged Rosa to step up onto the stage with a bow. She took the microphone from Jorge, who gave her a hug.

"I'm honored to announce that the blue roses will be known as Rosas Jacquis."

The sheet dropped dramatically to reveal the first blue rose preserved in glass with a gold plaque that stated: *Rosas Jacquis*. Rosa gestured to her grandmother as the crowd applauded.

"I love you, Abuela," Rose said.

Abuela Jacqui blew her a kiss and smiled peacefully. Pulling out a blue rose petal from her pocket, she began to chew it.

Jorge leaned toward the microphone, still in Rosa's hands. "That's enough from us. It's time to celebrate. Let's dance!"

The crowd cheered once more as a band behind them struck up a lively tune. Jorge began the dance with Rosa, and the workers all followed their lead.

Arturo clapped in time with the music as Rolando approached.

"Hey, gomelo. I wanted to thank you for your example. You laid it all out for Rosa, and I think it's time that I did the same for Bella. I'm gonna tell her how I really feel."

As he finished speaking, a beautiful woman, the dancer Arturo saw Rolando with earlier, stepped out from behind him. She was holding Rolando's hand.

"Wait! Rolando! Are you sure this is the best place to..."

"Absolutely, bro. This is gonna be awesome," Rolando bragged.

He ran off with a beaming smile, still holding the dancer's hand and ignoring the horrified look on Arturo's face. The pair climbed up on the stage so that Rolando could take the microphone.

"Excuse me! Can I have your attention, please?" He asked.

The music faded, and the dancing ended. All eyes were on Rolando.

"Bella Vasquez, will you join me up here? Bring the kids."

Arturo winced. This was going to be even worse than he had feared. He shook his head. "No, no, no, what are you doing?"

Bella proceeded up the steps, looking quite confused. "What's going on, Rolando?"

The dancer walked up to her and passed out sunglasses to the kids. Then she stepped behind them to give Rolando and Bella a clear path. She signaled the band to begin a new song.

Rolando approached his wife and took her hand. "Bella, years ago, you danced into my life. You were a vision and there I was – a chubby, great-smelling guy with an embarrassing lack of rhythm. Nevertheless, you still loved me, and every single day my happiness increases because of you."

The kids lined up behind him, all wearing sunglasses.

"I know life has been hard, but you have stayed with me through all the ups and downs, and I want to show you how much you mean to me," Rolando continued.

"Rolando?" Bella was even more confused.

He pressed a finger to her lips and popped on his sunglasses. "Here, my love is the greatest love song ever written." He turned to the dancer. "Hit it."

The dancer signaled the band, and it began to play the song as Rolando started a dance routine. He was fully committed, dancing like a fool in front of all their friends and family as Bella watched in dumbstruck awe. Then he popped and held out his hand to his wife.

"Rolando, you're an idiot," she said with a smile as she joined him.

They spun and moved and gyrated together, Bella just as committed as Rolando. The crowd joined in. It was like a big silly dance party. It was glorious. By the time the song ended with a deep bow and a kiss, Rolando and Bella were both sweating but happy.

"That was smooth, Buñuelo," Bella said. "Let's get someone to watch the kids so I can give you my present." She laughed. "Where did this come from?"

"Well, I was talking to Arturo and... Hey, where's Arturo?" he asked, looking around.

***

A mild breeze carried the music through the air, but it was much softer in the distance as Arturo and Rosa danced close together, alone by the lake. When the song was finished, he stepped back to a tree where he pulled out a single red rose and held it out to her.

"I have wanted to give you this for a long time," he said softly.

Rosa smiled. Taking it, she held it to her chest. "There's something I have wanted to do for a long time, too."

"Yeah? What's that?"

Rosa laughed and then ran toward the lake to splash in the water. Arturo followed, joining her. Picking her up, he spun her on his shoulders as the couple laughed and splashed like a couple of kids.

At a nearby tree, a young blue rose grew on the lakeside. The red rose lay next to it. They made a beautiful pair. As their laughter echoed across the lake, Rosa and Arturo knew that their lives would never be the same again. No more loneliness, no more searching. Just many years ahead filled with love, happiness, and joy.

www.ingramcontent.com/pod-product-compliance
Lightning Source LLC
Chambersburg PA
CBHW022037170626
46808CB00003B/1249

*9 7 8 1 7 3 4 7 6 9 6 5 4 *